Faerie

JUN 2 6 2005

Classics for Young Readers

Sir Gibbie by George Macdonald

Sir Gibbie: A Guide for Teachers and Students

Hans Brinker by Mary Mapes Dodge

Hans Brinker: A Guide for Teachers and Students

A Little Princess by Frances Hodgson Burnett

A Little Princess: A Guide for Teachers and Students

Black Beauty by Anna Sewell

Black Beauty: A Guide for Teachers and Students

Robinson Crusoe by Daniel Defoe

Robinson Crusoe: A Guide for Teachers and Students

Little Women by Louisa May Alcott

Little Women: A Guide for Teachers and Students

Faerie Gold: Treasures from the Lands of Enchantment

Faerie Gold: A Guide for Teachers and Students

Faerie Gold

Treasures from the
Lands of Enchantment

Edited by

Kathryn Lindskoog

and

Ranelda Mack Hunsicker

P U B L I S H I N G
P.O. BOX 817 • PHILLIPSBURG • NEW JERSEY 08865-0817

Page design by Tobias Design
Typesetting by Andrew MacBride

Printed in the United States of America

Library of Congress Cataloging-in-Publication Data

Faerie gold : treasures from the lands of enchantment / edited by Kathryn
Lindskoog and Ranelda Mack Hunsicker.
   p. cm.—(Classics for young readers)
   Contents: Little daylight / by George MacDonald—The fairy's new year gift / by Emilie Poulsson—Prince Cherry / by Dinah Mulock Craik—Kenneth and the carp / by Edith Nesbit—The skipping shoes / by Louisa May Alcott—The enchanted necklace / by Annie Fellows Johnston—The gold-bearded man / by Andrew Lang—The princess of the golden castle / by Katherine Pyle—The gate of the giant scissors / by Annie Fellows Johnston—The greedy shepherd / by Frances Browne—Flora's birthday party / Christina Rosetti—A lost paradise / by Andrew Lang—Justnowland / by Edith Nesdbit—The conceited apple-branch / by Hans Christian Andersen—A handful of clay / by Henry Van Dyke—The nightingale / by Andrew Lang—A Christmas Star / by Katherine Pyle—The coming of the king / by Laura E. Richards—The castle / by George MacDonald—The loveliest rose in the world / by Hans Christian Andersen / Robin Redbreast / by Selma Lagerlof.
   Summary: Presents twenty-one fairy tales and fantasy stories, selected to stimulate imagination and direct it toward God.
   ISBN 0-87552-738-8 (pbk.)
   1. Children's stories. [1. Fairy tales. 2. Fantasy. 3. Short stories.] I. Lindskoog, Kathryn, 1934– II. Hunsicker, Ranelda Mack, 1953– III. Series.

PZ5.F175 2005
[Fic]—dc22
                         2004057340

Contents

Introduction: Your Golden Key   7

Part One: Fairy Gifts   11

1. Little Daylight *by George MacDonald*   13
2. The Fairy's New Year Gift *by Emilie Poulsson*   38
3. Prince Cherry *by Dinah Mulock Craik*   41

Part Two: Magical Wishes   55

4. Kenneth and the Carp *by Edith Nesbit*   57
5. The Skipping Shoes *by Louisa May Alcott*   80
6. The Enchanted Necklace *by Annie Fellows Johnston*   92

Part Three: Clever Heroes   101

7. The Gold-Bearded Man *by Andrew Lang*   103
8. The Princess of the Golden Castle *by Katherine Pyle*   117
9. The Gate of the Giant Scissors *by Annie Fellows Johnston*   131

Part Four: Just Rewards   145

10. The Greedy Shepherd *by Frances Browne*   147

11. Flora's Birthday Party *by Christina Rossetti*   156

12. A Lost Paradise *by Andrew Lang*   175

13. Justnowland *by E. Nesbit*   181

Part Five: Nature's Wonders   199

14. The Conceited Apple-Branch *by Hans Christian Andersen*   201

15. A Handful of Clay *by Henry Van Dyke*   207

16. The Nightingale *by Hans Christian Andersen*   211

Part Six: Heavenly Marvels   223

17. A Christmas Star *by Katherine Pyle*   225

18. The Coming of the King *by Laura E. Richards*   232

19. The Castle *by George MacDonald*   235

20. The Loveliest Rose in the World *by Hans Christian Andersen*   252

21. Robin Redbreast *by Selma Lagerlöf*   256

A Message to Parents & Teachers:
Why Do We Need Fairy Tales and Fantasy?   265

Great Thoughts about Faerie and Fantasy:
A Quotation Collection   277

Authors Featured in *Faerie Gold*   287

INTRODUCTION
Your Golden Key

If I gave you a sheet of drawing paper and a set of colored pens, how would you use them?

Or if you were on a sandy beach with a shovel and bucket, what would you do?

And if you had to lie in bed very still for several hours—without books or television, music or a computer—where would you go in your mind?

The answer to each of these questions depends on you and a special power you possess . . . the power of imagination. Before we can create anything, we have to imagine it. And what we imagine comes from the deepest place inside us.

Where did we get this amazing ability to picture things our

eyes cannot see? To find out, we need to turn to the greatest story of all. There we read that, once upon a time, God imagined our world. And then He made it so. He pictured people like you and me, and He breathed life into us. He wanted to share the joy of making things and seeing that they are good. So He planted a tiny seed of His creativity in our hearts.

Every time someone tells a story, imagination is at work. Without leaving our chairs, we travel through time and space. And when we enter the enchanted kingdom called Faerie—whether or not we find any fairies—we see the world in brand-new ways. Old, everyday things like wardrobes and mirrors and wells take us where we have never been. We never know what to expect around each corner and turn in the road.

Between the covers of this book are many gateways to magical places. Go where you like and leave when you want to. Take the doors you choose in any order you wish.

But whenever you venture into Faerie, remember that the world of imagination is a dangerous place filled with giants and ogres and dragons, as well as magic wishes and thrilling adventures. Here is how J. R. R. Tolkien, author of *The Lord of the Rings*, describes it: "The land of fairy-story is wide and deep and high, and is filled with many things: all manner of beasts and birds are found there; shoreless seas and stars uncounted; beauty that is enchantment, and an ever-present peril; both sorrow and joy as sharp as swords."

To make it safely through the lands of enchantment, you will need:

> A light to guide your path,
> A sword to battle evil, and
> A shield to guard your heart.

All three of these gifts can be yours from the same One who gave you the golden key of imagination. Use them wisely as you explore the kingdom of the fairies.

PART ONE

FAIRY GIFTS

For every child should understand
That letters from the first were planned
To guide us into Fairy Land.
So labor at your Alphabet,
For by that learning shall you get
To lands where Fairies may be met.
And going where this pathway goes,
You too, at last, may find, who knows?
The Garden of the Singing Rose.

—**Andrew Lang,** *The Yellow Fairy Book*

ONE
Little Daylight

by George MacDonald

from *At the Back of the North Wind* (1871)

No house is in the least worthy to be called a palace without a wood near it—very near it—and the nearer the better. Not all round it—I don't mean that, for a palace ought to be open to the sun and wind, and stand high and brave, with weathercocks glittering and flags flying; but on one side of every palace there must be a wood. And there was a very grand wood indeed beside the palace of the king who was going to be Daylight's father; such a grand wood, that nobody yet had ever got to the other end of it. Near the house it was kept very trim and nice, and it was free of brushwood for a long way in; but by degrees it got wild, and it grew wilder, and wilder, and wilder, until some said wild beasts at last did what they liked in it. The king and his noblemen often hunted, however, and this kept the wild beasts far away from the palace.

One glorious summer morning, when the wind and sun were out together, when the flags were frolicking against the blue sky, little Daylight made her appearance—a beautiful baby, with such bright eyes that she might have come from the sun, only by and by she showed such lively ways that she might equally well have come out of the wind. There was great jubilation in the palace, for this was the first baby the queen had had, and there is as much happiness over a new baby in a palace as in a cottage.

But there is one disadvantage of living near a wood: you do not know quite who your neighbors may be. Everybody knew there were in it several fairies, living within a few miles of the palace, who always had had something to do with each new baby that came; for fairies live so much longer than we, that they can have business with a good many generations of human mortals. The curious houses they lived in were well known also—one, a hollow oak; another, a birch-tree, though nobody could ever find how that fairy made a house of it; another, a hut of growing trees intertwined, and patched up with turf and moss. But there was another fairy who had lately come to the place, and nobody even knew she was a fairy except the other fairies. A wicked old thing she was, always hiding her power, and being as disagreeable as she could, in order to tempt people to give her offence, that she might have the pleasure of taking vengeance upon them. People thought she was a witch, and those who knew her by sight were careful to avoid offending her. She lived in a mud house, in a swampy part of the forest.

In all history we find that fairies give their remarkable gifts to prince or princess, or any child of sufficient importance in their eyes, at the christening. Now this we can understand, because it is an ancient custom among human beings as well, and it is not hard to explain why wicked fairies should choose the same time to do unkind things; but it is difficult to understand how they should be able to do them, for you would fancy all wicked creatures would be powerless on such an occasion. But I never knew of any interference on the part of the wicked fairy that did not turn out a good thing in the end. What a good thing, for instance, it was that one princess should sleep for a hundred years! Was she not saved from all the plague of young men who were not worthy of her? And did she not come awake exactly at the right moment when the right prince kissed her? For my part, I cannot help wishing a good many girls would sleep till just the same fate overtook them. It would be happier for them, and more agreeable to their friends.

All the known fairies were invited to the christening. But the king and queen never thought of inviting an old witch. For the power of the fairies they have by nature; but a witch gets her power by wickedness.

Of course, the old hag was there without being asked. Not to be asked was just what she wanted, that she might have a sort of reason for doing what she wished to do. For, somehow, even the wickedest of creatures likes an excuse for doing the wrong thing.

Five fairies had one after the other given the child such gifts as each counted best, and the fifth had just stepped back to her place in the surrounding splendor of ladies and gentlemen, when, mumbling a laugh between her toothless gums, the wicked fairy hobbled out into the middle of the circle. At the moment when the archbishop was handing the baby to the lady at the head of the nursery department, the wicked fairy addressed him thus, giving a bite or two to every word before she could part with it:

"Please your Grace, I'm very deaf: would your Grace mind repeating the princess's name?"

"With pleasure, my good woman," said the archbishop, stooping to shout in her ear: "the infant's name is little Daylight."

"And little Daylight it shall be," cried the fairy, in the tone of a dry axle, "and little good shall any of her gifts do her. For I bestow upon her the gift of sleeping all day long, whether she will or not. Ha, ha! He, he! Hi, hi!"

Then out started the sixth fairy. The others had arranged she should come after the wicked one, in order to undo as much as she might.

"If she sleep all day," she said, sadly, "she shall, at least, wake all night."

"A nice prospect for her mother and me!" thought the poor king; for they loved her far too much to give her up to nurses, as most kings and queens do—and are sorry for it afterwards.

"You spoke before I had done," said the wicked fairy. "That's against the law. It gives me another chance."

"I beg your pardon," said the other fairies, all together.

"She did. I hadn't done laughing," said the crone. "I had only got to Hi, hi! and I had to go through Ho, ho! and Hu, hu! So I decree that if she wakes all night she shall wax and wane with its mistress, the moon. And what that may mean I hope her royal parents will live to see. Ho, ho! Hu, hu!"

But out stepped another fairy, for they had been wise enough to keep two in reserve, because every fairy knew the trick of one.

"Until," said the seventh fairy, "a prince comes who shall kiss her without knowing it."

The wicked fairy made a horrid noise like an angry cat and hobbled away. She could not pretend that she had not finished her speech this time, for she had laughed Ho, ho! and Hu, hu!

"I don't know what that means," said the poor king to the seventh fairy.

"Don't be afraid. The meaning will come with the thing itself," said she.

The assembly broke up, miserable enough—the queen, at least, prepared for a good many sleepless nights, and the lady at the head of the nursery department anything but comfortable in the prospect before her, for of course the queen could not do it all. As for the king, he made up his mind, with what courage he could summon, to meet the demands of the case, but wondered whether he could with any propriety require the First Lord of the Treasury to take a share in the burden laid upon him.

I will not attempt to describe what they had to go through for some time. But at last the household settled into a regular system—a very irregular one in some respects. For at certain seasons the palace rang all night with bursts of laughter from little Daylight, whose heart the old fairy's curse could not reach; she was Daylight still, only a little in the wrong place, for she always dropped asleep at the first hint of dawn in the east. But her merriment was of short duration. When the moon was at the full, she was in glorious spirits, and as beautiful as it was possible for a child of her age to be. But as the moon waned, she faded, until at last she looked like the poorest, sickliest child you might come upon in the streets of a great city in the arms of a homeless mother. Then the night was quiet as the day, for the little creature lay in her gorgeous cradle night and day with hardly a motion, and at last without even a moan, like one dead. At first they often thought she was dead, but at last they got used to it, and only consulted the almanac to find the moment when she would begin to revive, which, of course, was with the first appearance of the silver thread of the crescent moon. Then she would move her lips, and they would give her a little nourishment, and she would grow better and better and better, until for a few days she was splendidly well. When well, she was always merriest out in the moonlight, but even when near her worst, she seemed better when, in warm summer nights, they carried her cradle out into the light of the waning moon. Then in her sleep she would smile the faintest, most pitiful smile.

For a long time very few people ever saw her awake. As she grew older she became such a favorite, however, that about the palace there were always some who would arrange to stay awake at night, in order to be near her. But she soon began to take every chance of getting away from her nurses and enjoying her moonlight alone. And thus things went on until she was nearly seventeen years of age. Her father and mother had by that time got so used to the odd state of things that they had ceased to wonder at them. All their arrangements depended on the state of the Princess Daylight. But how any prince was ever to find and deliver her, seemed impossible to imagine.

As she grew older she had grown more and more beautiful, with the sunniest hair and the loveliest eyes of heavenly blue, brilliant and deep as the sky of a June day. But so much more painful and sad was the change as her bad time came on. The more beautiful she was in the full moon, the more withered and worn did she become as the moon waned. At the time at which my story has now arrived, she looked, when the moon was small or gone, like an old woman exhausted with suffering. This was more painful and unnatural because her hair and eyes did not change. Her pale face was both drawn and wrinkled, and had an eager hungry look. Her skinny hands moved as if wishing, but unable, to lay hold of something. Her shoulders were bent forward, her chest went in, and she stooped as if she were eighty years old. At last she had to be put to bed, and there await the flow of the tide of life. But she grew to dislike being seen, still more being touched by any hands, during this season. One lovely summer evening, when the moon lay all but gone upon the verge of the horizon, she vanished from her attendants, and it was only after searching for her a long time in great terror that they found her fast asleep in the forest, at the foot of a silver birch tree, and carried her home.

A little way from the palace there was a great open glade, covered with the greenest and softest grass. This was her favorite place; for here the full moon shone free and glorious, and through the trees she could generally see the dying moon as it crossed the opening. Here she had a little rustic house built for her, and here she mostly resided. None of the court might go there without leave, and her own attendants had learned by this time not to be bossy in waiting upon her, so that she was very much at liberty. Whether the good fairies had anything to do with it or not I cannot tell, but at last she got into the habit of retreating further into the wood every night as the moon waned, so that sometimes her attendants had great trouble in finding her; but as she was always very angry if she discovered they were watching her, they scarcely dared to do so. At length one night they thought they had lost her altogether. It was morning before they found her. Feeble as she was, she had wandered into a thicket a long way from the glade, and there she lay—fast asleep, of course.

Although the fame of her beauty and sweetness had gone abroad, everybody knew she was under a bad spell. As a result, no king in the neighborhood had any desire to have her for a daughter-in-law.

About this time in a neighboring kingdom, because of the wickedness of the nobles, a revolution took place upon the death of the old king. Most of the nobles were massacred, and the young prince was forced to run for his life, disguised like a peasant. For some time, until he got out of the country, he suffered much from hunger and fatigue, but when he got into the country ruled by Princess Daylight's father, and had no longer any fear of being recognized, he fared better, for the people were kind. He did not abandon his disguise, however. One reason was that he had no other clothes to put on, and another that he had very little money, and did not know where to get any more. There was no good in telling everybody he met that he was a prince, for he felt that a prince ought to be able to get on like other people, or else his rank only made a fool of him. He had read of princes setting out upon adventure, and here he was out in a similar way, only without having had a choice in the matter. He would go on, and see what would come of it.

For a day or two he had been walking through the palace-wood, and had had next to nothing to eat. Then he came upon the strangest little house, inhabited by a very nice, tidy, motherly old woman. This was one of the good fairies. The moment she saw him she knew quite well who he was and what was going to come of it; but she was not free to interfere with the orderly march of events. She received him with the kindness she would have shown to any other traveler, and gave him bread and milk, which he thought the most delicious food he had ever tasted. The old woman insisted he stay all night. When he awoke he was amazed to find how well and strong he felt. She would not take any of the money he offered, but begged him, if he found reasons to stay in the neighborhood, to return to her house.

"Thank you much, good mother," answered the prince, "but there is little chance of that. The sooner I get out of this wood the better."

"I don't know that," said the fairy.

"What do you mean?" asked the prince.

"Why, how should I know?" returned she.

"I can't tell," said the prince.

"Very well," said the fairy.

"How strangely you talk!" said the prince.

"Do I?" said the fairy.

"Yes, you do," said the prince.

"Very well," said the fairy.

The prince was not used to being spoken to in this fashion, so he felt a little angry, and turned and walked away. But this did not offend the fairy. She stood at the door of her little house looking after him till the trees hid him quite. Then she said "At last!" and went in.

The prince wandered and wandered, and got nowhere. The sun sank and sank and went out of sight, and he seemed no nearer the end of the wood than ever. He sat down on a fallen tree, ate a bit of bread the old woman had given him, and waited for the moon; for, although he was not much of an astronomer, he knew the moon would rise sometime. Up she came, slow and slow, but of a good size, pretty nearly round indeed. Then, greatly refreshed with his piece of bread, he got up and went—he knew not where.

After walking a considerable distance, he thought he was coming to the outside of the forest, but when he reached what he thought was the last of it, he found himself only upon the edge of a great open space in it, covered with grass. The moon shone very bright, and he thought he had never seen a more lovely spot. Still it looked dreary because of its loneliness, for he could not see the house at the other side. He sat down, weary again, and gazed into the glade. He had not seen so much room for several days.

All at once he spied something in the middle of the grass. What could it be? It moved; it came nearer. Was it a human creature, gliding across—a girl dressed in white, gleaming in the moonshine? She came nearer and nearer. He crept behind a tree and watched, wondering. It must be some strange being of the wood—a nymph whom the moonlight and the warm dusky air had enticed from her tree. But when she came close to where he stood, he no longer doubted she was human—for he had caught sight of her sunny hair, and her clear blue eyes, and the loveliest face and form that he had ever seen. All at once she began singing like a nightingale, and dancing to her own music, with her eyes ever turned towards the moon. She passed close to where he stood, dancing on by the edge of the trees and away in a great circle towards the other side, until he could see only a spot of white in the yellowish green of the moonlit grass. But when he feared it would vanish completely, the spot grew, and became a figure once more. She approached him again, singing and dancing, and waving her arms over her head, until she had completed the circle. Just opposite his tree she stood, ceased her song, dropped her arms, and broke out into a long clear laugh, musical as a brook. Then, as if tired, she threw herself on the grass, and lay gazing at the moon. The prince was almost afraid to breathe lest he should startle her, and she should vanish from his sight. As to venturing near her, that never came into his head.

She had lain for a long hour or longer, when the prince began again to doubt concerning her. Perhaps she was but a vision of his own fancy. Or was she a spirit of the wood, after all? If so, he too would haunt the wood, glad to have lost kingdom and everything for the hope of being near her. He would build him a hut in the forest, and there he would live for the pure chance of seeing her again. Upon nights like this at least she would come out and bask in the moonlight, and make his soul blessed. But while he thus dreamed she sprang to her feet, turned her face full to the moon, and began singing as if she would draw the moon down from the sky by the power of her enchanting voice. She looked more beautiful than ever. Again she began dancing to her own music, and danced away into the distance. Once more she returned in a similar manner, but although he was watching as eagerly as before, he became tired and fell fast asleep before she came near him. When he awoke it was broad daylight, and the princess was nowhere.

He could not leave the place. What if she should come the next night! He would gladly endure a day's hunger to see her yet again. He walked round the glade to see if he could discover any prints of her feet. But the grass was so short, and her steps had been so light that she had not left a single trace behind her. He walked halfway round the wood without seeing anything to account for her presence. Then he spied a lovely little house, with thatched roof and low eaves, surrounded by an exquisite garden, with doves and peacocks walking in it. Of course, this must be where the gracious lady who loved the moonlight lived. Forgetting his appearance, he walked towards the door, determined to make inquiries, but as he passed a little pond full of gold and silver fishes, he caught sight of himself and turned to find the door to the kitchen. There he knocked, and asked for a piece of bread. The good-natured cook brought him in and gave him an excellent breakfast, which the prince found nothing the worse for being served in the kitchen. While he ate, he talked with the cook and learned that this was the favorite retreat of the Princess Daylight. But he learned nothing more, both because he was afraid of seeming inquisitive, and because the cook did not choose to be heard talking about her mistress to a peasant lad who had begged for his breakfast.

As he rose to take his leave, it occurred to him that he might not be so far from the old woman's cottage as he had thought, and he asked the cook whether she knew anything of such a place, describing it as well as he could. She said she knew it well enough, adding with a smile, "It's there you're going, is it?"

"Yes, if it's not far off."

"It's not more than three miles. But be careful what you are about, you know."

"Why do you say that?"

"If you're after any mischief, she'll make you repent it."

"The best thing that could happen under the circumstances," remarked the prince.

"What do you mean by that?" asked the cook.

"Why, it stands to reason," answered the prince, "that if you wish to do anything wrong, the best thing for you is to be made to repent of it."

"I see," said the cook. "Well, I think you may venture. She's a good old soul."

"Which way does it lie from here?" asked the prince.

She gave him full instructions, and he left her with many thanks.

Now refreshed, however, the prince did not go back to the cottage that day; he remained in the forest, amusing himself as best he could, but waiting anxiously for the night, in the hope that the princess would again appear. Nor was he disappointed, for, as soon as the moon rose, he spied a glimmering shape far across the glade. As it drew nearer, he saw it was she indeed—dressed in pale blue like the sky, and she looked lovelier still. He thought it was because the blue suited her yet better than the white; he did not know that she was really more beautiful because the moon was nearer the full.

In fact, the next night was full moon, and the princess would then be at the zenith of her loveliness.

The prince feared for some time that she was not coming near his hiding-place that night; but the circles in her dance ever widened as the moon rose, until at last they embraced the whole glade, and she came still closer to the trees where he was hiding than she had come the night before. He was entranced with her loveliness, for it was indeed a marvelous thing. All night long he watched her, but dared not go near her. He would have been ashamed of watching her too, had he not become almost unable to think of anything but how beautiful she was. He watched the whole night long, and he saw that as the moon went down she retreated in smaller and smaller circles, until at last he could see her no more.

Weary as he was, he set out for the old woman's cottage. He arrived just in time for her breakfast, which she shared with him. He then went to bed and slept for many hours. When he awoke the sun was down, and he departed in great anxiety lest he should lose a glimpse of the lovely vision. But, whether it was by the scheming of the swamp-fairy, or merely that it is one thing to go and another to return by the same road, he lost his way. I shall not attempt to describe his misery when the moon rose, and he saw nothing but trees, trees, trees.

The moon was high in the heavens before he reached the glade. Then, indeed, his troubles vanished, for there was the princess dancing towards him in a dress that shone like gold, and with shoes that glimmered through the grass like fireflies. She was still more beautiful than before. Like a sunbeam come to life, she passed him, and danced away into the distance.

Before she returned in her circle, the clouds had begun to gather about the moon. The wind rose, the trees moaned, and their lighter branches leaned all one way before it. The prince feared that the princess would go in, and he should see her no more that night. But she came dancing on, more jubilant than ever. Her golden dress and her sunny hair streamed out upon the blast, and she waved her arms towards the moon, seeming to order the clouds away from her face. The prince could hardly believe she was not a creature of the elements, after all.

By the time she had completed another circle, the clouds had gathered deep, and there were growlings of distant thunder. Just as she passed the tree where he stood, a flash of lightning blinded him for a moment, and when he saw again, to his horror, the princess lay on the ground. He darted to her, thinking she had been struck, but when she heard him coming, she was on her feet in a moment.

"What do you want?" she asked.

"I beg your pardon. I thought—the lightning," said the prince, hesitating.

"There's nothing the matter," said the princess, waving him off rather haughtily.

The poor prince turned and walked towards the wood.

"Come back," said Daylight. "I like you. You do what you are told. Are you good?"

"Not so good as I should like to be," said the prince.

"Then go and grow better," said the princess.

Again the disappointed prince turned and went.

"Come back," said the princess.

He obeyed, and stood before her waiting.

"Can you tell me what the sun is like?" she asked.

"No," he answered. "But where's the good of asking what you know?"

"But I don't know," she said.

"Why, everybody knows."

"That's the very thing: I'm not everybody. I've never seen the sun."

"Then you can't know what it's like till you do see it."

"I think you must be a prince," said the princess.

"Do I look like one?" said the prince.

"I can't quite say that."

"Then why do you think so?"

"Because you both do what you are told and speak the truth.—Is the sun so very bright?"

"As bright as the lightning."

"But it doesn't go out like that, does it?"

"Oh, no. It shines like the moon, rises and sets like the moon, is much the same shape as the moon, only so bright that you can't look at it for a moment."

"But I would look at it," said the princess.

"But you couldn't," said the prince.

"But I could," said the princess.

"Why don't you, then?"

"Because I can't."

"Why can't you?"

"Because I can't wake. And I never shall wake until—"

Here she hid her face in her hands, turned away, and walked in the slowest, stateliest manner towards the house. The prince dared to follow her at a little distance, but she turned and made a gesture for him to stop, which, like a true gentleman-prince, he obeyed at once. He waited a long time, but as she did not come near him again, and as the night had now cleared, he set off at last for the old woman's cottage.

It was long past midnight when he reached it, but, to his surprise, the old woman was cutting potatoes at the door. Fairies are fond of doing odd things. Indeed, the night is always their day. And so it is with all who have fairy blood in them.

"Why, what are you doing there, this time of the night, mother?" said the prince; for that was the kind way in which any young man in his country would address a woman who was much older than himself.

"Getting your supper ready, my son," she answered.

"Oh, I don't want any supper," said the prince.

"Ah! you've seen Daylight," said she.

"I've seen a princess who never saw it," said the prince.

"Do you like her?" asked the fairy.

"Oh, yes!" said the prince. "More than you would believe, mother."

"A fairy can believe anything that ever was or ever could be," said the old woman.

"Then are you a fairy?" asked the prince. "Do you believe there could be a princess who never saw the daylight?"

The prince believed it, but he hoped the fairy would tell him more. She was too old a fairy, however, to be caught so easily.

"Of all people, fairies must not tell secrets. Besides, she's a princess."

"Well, I'll tell you a secret. I'm a prince."

"I know that."

"How do you know it?"

"By the curl of the third eyelash on your left eyelid."

"Which corner do you count from?"

"That's a secret."

"Another secret? Well, at least, if I am a prince, there can be no harm in telling me about a princess."

"It's just the princess I can't tell."

He could get nothing more out of the fairy, and had to go to bed with his questions unanswered, which was something of a trial.

Now wicked fairies will not be bound by the law which

the good fairies obey, and this always seems to give the bad the advantage over the good, for they use means to gain their ends which the others will not. But it is all of no consequence, for what they do never succeeds; nay, in the end it brings about the very thing they are trying to prevent. So you see that somehow, for all their cleverness, wicked fairies are dreadfully stupid, for, although from the beginning of the world they have really helped instead of stopping the good fairies, not one of them is a bit wiser for it. She will try the bad thing just as they all did before her, and succeed no better, of course.

The swamp-fairy did not know the prince was in the neighborhood until after he had seen the princess those three times. When she knew it, she comforted herself by thinking that the princess must be far too proud and too modest for any young man to venture even to speak to her before he had seen her six times at least. But there was even less danger than the wicked fairy thought; for, however much the princess might desire to be set free, she was dreadfully afraid of the wrong prince. Now, however, the fairy was going to do all she could.

She so contrived it by her deceitful spells that the next night the prince could not find his way to the glade. It would take me too long to tell her tricks. They would be amusing to us, who know that they could not do any harm, but they were something other than amusing to the poor prince. He wandered about the forest till daylight, and then fell fast asleep. The same thing happened for seven days, during which he also could not find the good fairy's cottage. After the third quarter of the moon, however, the bad fairy thought she might be at ease for two weeks at least, for there was no chance of the prince wishing to kiss the princess during that period.

The first day of the fourth quarter he did find the cottage, and the next day he found the glade. For nearly another week he stayed near it. But the princess never came. I have little doubt she was on the farther edge of it some part of every night, but at this period she always wore black, and, with little or no light, the prince never saw her. Nor would he have known her if he had seen her. How could he have taken the weak and worn creature she was now for the glorious Princess Daylight?

At last, one night when there was no moon at all, he ventured near the house. There he heard voices talking, although it was past midnight. The princess's attendants were uneasy because the one whose turn it was to watch her had fallen asleep and had not seen which way she went. They knew this was a night when she would probably wander very far, making a circle which did not touch the open glade at all, but stretched away from the back of the house, deep into that side of the forest—a part of which the prince knew nothing. When he understood from what they said that she had disappeared, he plunged at once into the wood to see if he could find her. For hours he roamed with nothing to guide him but the vague notion of a circle, which on one side bordered on the house, for so much had he picked up from the talk he had overheard.

It was getting towards the dawn, but as yet there was no streak of light in the sky, when he came to a great birch tree, and sat down weary at the foot of it. While he sat—very miserable, you may be sure—full of fear for the princess, and wondering how her attendants could take it so quietly, he decided that it would not be a bad plan to light a fire. If she were anywhere near, it would attract her. This he managed with a tinderbox, which the good fairy had given him. It was just beginning to blaze up when he heard a moan. It seemed to come from the other side of the tree. He sprang to his feet, but his heart throbbed so that he had to lean for a moment against the tree before he could move. When he got round, there lay a human form in a little dark heap on the earth. There was light enough from his fire to show that it was not the princess. He lifted it in his arms, hardly heavier than a child, and carried it to the flame. The face was that of an old woman, but it had a fearfully strange look. A black hood concealed her hair, and her eyes were closed. He laid her down as comfortably as he could, rubbed her hands, put a little cordial from a bottle—also the gift of the fairy— into her mouth; took off his coat and wrapped it about her, and in short did the best he could. In a little while she opened her eyes and looked at him—so pitifully! The tears rose and flowed from her gray wrinkled cheeks, but she said never a word. She closed her eyes again, but the tears kept on flowing, and her whole appearance was so utterly pitiful that the prince was near crying too. He begged her to tell him what was the matter, promising to do all he could to help her, but still she did not speak. He thought she was dying, and he took her in his arms again to carry her to the princess's house, where he thought the good-natured cook might be able to do something for her. When he lifted her, the tears flowed yet faster, and she gave such a sad moan that it went to his very heart.

"Mother, mother!" he said. "Poor mother!" and kissed her on the withered lips.

She started, and what eyes they were that opened upon him! But he did not see them, for it was still very dark, and he had enough to do to make his way through the trees towards the house.

Just as he approached the door, feeling more tired than he could have imagined possible, she began to move and became so restless that, unable to carry her a moment longer, he thought to lay her on the grass. But she stood upright on her feet. Her hood had dropped, and her hair fell about her. The first gleam of the morning was caught on her face: that face was bright as the never-aging Dawn, and her eyes were lovely as the sky of darkest blue. The prince drew back in overwhelming wonder. It was Daylight herself whom he had brought from the forest! He fell at her feet, not daring to look up until she laid her hand upon his head. He rose then.

"You kissed me when I was an old woman. There! I kiss you when I am a young princess," murmured Daylight. "—Is that the sun coming?"

TWO

The Fairy's New Year Gift

by Emilie Poulsson

from *In the Child's World* (1893)
adapted by Frances J. Olcott in *Good Stories for Great Holidays* (1914)

Two little boys were at play one day when a Fairy suddenly appeared before them and said: "I have been sent to give you New Year presents."

She handed to each child a package, and in an instant was gone.

Carl and Philip opened the packages and found in them two beautiful books, with pages as pure and white as the snow when it first falls.

Many months passed and the Fairy came again to the boys. "I have brought you each another book," said she, "and will take the first ones back to Father Time who sent them to you."

"May I not keep mine a little longer?" asked Philip. "I have hardly thought about it lately. I'd like to paint something on the last leaf that lies open."

"No," said the Fairy. "I must take it just as it is."

"I wish that I could look through mine just once," said Carl. "I have only seen one page at a time, for when the leaf turns over it sticks fast, and I can never open the book at more than one place each day."

"You shall look at your book," said the Fairy, "and Philip, at his." And she lit for them two little silver lamps, by the light of which they saw the pages as she turned them.

The boys looked in wonder. Could it be that these were the same fair books she had given them a year ago? Where were the clean, white pages, as pure and beautiful as the snow when it first falls? Here was a page with ugly, black spots and scratches upon it; while the very next page showed a lovely little picture. Some pages were decorated with gold and silver and gorgeous colors, others with beautiful flowers, and still others with a rainbow of softest, most delicate brightness. Yet even on the most beautiful of the pages there were ugly blots and scratches.

Carl and Philip looked up at the Fairy at last.

"Who did this?" they asked. "Every page was white and fair as we opened to it; yet now there is not a single blank place in the whole book!"

"Shall I explain some of the pictures to you?" said the Fairy, smiling at the two little boys.

"See, Philip, the spray of roses blossomed on this page when you let the baby have your playthings; and this pretty bird, that looks as if it were singing with all its might, would never have been on this page if you had not tried to be kind and pleasant the other day, instead of quarreling."

"But what makes this blot?" asked Philip.

"That," said the Fairy sadly, "that came when you told an untruth one day, and this when you did not mind Mamma. All these blots and scratches that look so ugly, both in your book and in Carl's, were made when you were naughty. Each pretty thing in your books came on its page when you were good."

"Oh, if we could only have the books again!" said Carl and Philip.

"That cannot be," said the Fairy. "See! They are dated for this year, and they must now go back into Father Time's book-case, but I have brought you each a new one. Perhaps you can make these more beautiful than the others."

So saying, she vanished, and the boys were left alone, but each held in his hand a new book open at the first page.

And on the back of this book was written in letters of gold, "For the New Year."

THREE

Prince Cherry

by Miss Mulock (Dinah Mulock Craik)

from *The Little Lame Prince* (1874)

Long ago there lived a monarch, who was such a very honest man that his subjects called him the Good King. One day, when he was out hunting, a little white rabbit, which had been half-killed by his hounds, leaped right into his majesty's arms. Caressing it, he said, "This poor creature has put itself under my protection, and I will allow no one to injure it." So he carried it to his palace, had prepared for it a neat little rabbit hutch, with plenty of food, such as rabbits love, and there he left it.

The same night, when he was alone in his chamber, there appeared to him a beautiful lady. She was dressed neither in gold, nor silver, nor brocade, but her flowing robes were white as snow, and she wore a garland of white roses on her head. The Good King was greatly astonished at the sight; for his door was locked, and he wondered how so dazzling a lady could possibly enter, but she soon removed his doubts.

"I am the fairy Candide," said she, with a smiling and gracious air. "Passing through the wood where you were hunting, I decided to find out if you were as good as men say you are. So I changed myself into a white rabbit and took refuge in your arms. You saved me and now I know that those who are merciful to animals will be ten times more so to human beings. You deserve the name your subjects give you: you are the Good King. I thank you for your protection and shall be always one of your best friends. You have but to say what you most desire, and I promise you your wish shall be granted."

"Madam," replied the king, "if you are a fairy, you must know, without my telling you, the wish of my heart. I have one beloved son, Prince Cherry. Whatever kindly feeling you have toward me, extend it to him."

"Willingly," said Candide. "I will make him the handsomest, richest, or most powerful prince in the world. Choose whichever you desire for him."

"None of the three," returned the father. "I only wish him to be good—the best prince in the whole world. Of what use would riches, power, or beauty be to him if he were a bad man?"

"You are right," said the fairy, "but I cannot make him

good. He must do that himself. I can only change his external fortunes; for his personal character, the most I can promise is to give him good counsel, reprove him for his faults, and even punish him, if he will not punish himself. You mortals can do the same with your children."

"Ah, yes!" said the king, sighing. Still, he felt that the kindness of a fairy was something gained for his son, and he died not long after, content and at peace.

Prince Cherry mourned deeply, for he dearly loved his father. He would have gladly given all his kingdoms and treasures to keep him in life a little longer. Two days after the Good King was no more, Prince Cherry was sleeping in his chamber when he saw the same dazzling vision of the fairy Candide.

"I promised your father," said she, "to be your best friend, and in pledge of this take what I now give you." She placed a small gold ring upon his finger. "Poor as it looks, it is more precious than diamonds; for whenever you do ill it will prick your finger. If, after that warning, you still continue in evil, you will lose my friendship, and I shall become your worst enemy."

So saying, she disappeared, leaving Cherry in such amazement that he would have believed it all a dream, except for the ring on his finger.

For a long time he was so good that the ring never pricked him at all. This made him so cheerful and pleasant in his humor that everybody called him "Happy Prince Cherry." But one unlucky day he was out hunting and found no game, which annoyed him so much that he showed his ill temper by his looks and ways. He imagined his ring felt very tight and uncomfortable, but as it did not prick him he paid no attention until, reentering his palace, his little pet dog, Bibi, jumped upon him and was sharply told to get away. The creature, accustomed to nothing but caresses, tried to attract his attention by pulling at his garments. Prince Cherry turned and gave Bibi a severe kick. At this moment he felt in his finger a prick like a pin.

"What nonsense!" he said to himself. "The fairy must be making game of me. Why, what great evil have I done! I, the master of a great empire, cannot I kick my own dog?"

A voice replied, or else Prince Cherry imagined it, "No, sire, the master of a great empire has a right to do good, but not evil. I—a fairy—am as much above you as you are above your dog. I might punish you, kill you, if I chose; but I prefer leaving you to amend your ways. You have been guilty of three faults today—bad temper, passion, cruelty. Do better tomorrow."

The prince promised, and kept his word a while; but he had been brought up by a foolish nurse, who indulged him in every way and was always telling him that he would be a king one day, when he might do as he liked in all things. When he found out that even a king cannot always do that, it made him angry. His ring began to prick him so often that his little finger was continually bleeding. At last, unable to put up with it any more, he took his ring off and hid it where he would never see it. Then he believed himself the happiest of men, for he could do exactly what he liked. He did it, and became every day more and more miserable.

One day he saw a beautiful young girl. Being always accustomed to have his own way, he immediately determined to marry her. He never doubted that she would be only too glad to be made a queen, for she was very poor. But Zelia—that was her name—answered, to his great astonishment, that she would rather not marry him.

"Do I displease you?" asked the prince, into whose mind it had never entered that he could displease anybody.

"Not at all, my prince," said the honest peasant maiden. "You are very handsome, very charming; but you are not like your father the Good King. I will not be your queen, for you would make me miserable."

At these words the prince's love seemed to turn to hatred. He gave orders to his guards to take Zelia to a prison near the palace, and then took counsel with his foster brother, the one of all his bad companions who most encouraged him to do wrong.

"Sir," said this man, "if I were in your majesty's place, I would never upset myself about a poor silly girl. Feed her on bread and water until she comes to her senses. If she still refuses you, let her die in torment, as a warning to your other subjects should they dare to challenge your will. You will be disgraced should you suffer yourself to be conquered by a simple girl."

"But," said Prince Cherry, "shall I not be disgraced if I harm a creature so perfectly innocent?"

"No one is innocent who disputes your majesty's authority," said the courtier, bowing. "It is better to commit an injustice than allow people to think you can ever be contradicted without punishment."

This touched Cherry on his weak point. His good impulses faded, and he decided to ask Zelia once more if she would marry him. If she again refused, he would sell her as a slave. When he arrived at the cell in which she was confined, he was astonished to find her gone! He knew not whom to accuse, for he had kept the key in his pocket the whole time. At last, the foster brother suggested that the escape of Zelia might have been arranged by an old man named Suliman. This man was the prince's former tutor and the only one who now ventured to blame him for anything that he did. Cherry sent immediately and ordered his old friend to be brought to him, loaded heavily with irons. Then, full of fury, he shut himself up in his own chamber, where he went raging to and fro, until startled by a noise like a clap of thunder. The fairy Candide stood before him.

"Prince," said she, in a severe voice, "I promised your father to give you good advice and to punish you if you refused to follow it. My counsel was forgotten, my punishment despised. Under the figure of a man, you have been no better than the beasts you chase: like a lion in fury, a wolf in gluttony, a serpent in revenge, and a bull in brutality. Take, therefore, in your new form the likeness of all these animals."

Scarcely had Prince Cherry heard these words than to his horror he found himself transformed into what the Fairy had named. He was a creature with the head of a lion, the horns of a bull, the feet of a wolf, and the tail of a serpent. At the same time he felt himself transported to a distant forest, where, standing on the bank of a stream, he saw reflected in the water his own frightful shape, and heard a voice saying, "Look at yourself, and know your soul has become a thousand times uglier even than your body."

Cherry recognized the voice of Candide, and in his rage would have sprung upon her and devoured her; but he saw nothing and the same voice said behind him, "Cease your feeble fury, and learn to conquer your pride by being in submission to your own subjects."

Hearing no more, he soon left the stream, hoping at least to get rid of the sight of himself. He had scarcely gone twenty paces when he tumbled into a pitfall that was laid to catch bears. The bear hunters, descending from some trees close by, caught him, chained him. Delighted to get hold of such a curious-looking animal, they led him along with them to the capital of his own kingdom.

There great rejoicing was taking place, and the bear hunters asked what it was all about. They were told that it was because Prince Cherry, the torment of his subjects, had just been struck dead by a thunderbolt—just punishment of all his crimes. Four of his wicked companions at court had wished to divide his throne between them, but the people had risen up against them and offered the crown to Suliman, the old tutor whom Cherry had ordered to be arrested.

All this the poor monster heard. He even saw Suliman sitting upon his throne and trying to calm the crowds by telling them that it was not certain Prince Cherry was dead, that he might return one day to reclaim with honor the crown which Suliman only agreed to wear as a sort of viceroy or representative of the prince.

"I know his heart," said the honest and faithful old man. "It is tainted, but not corrupt. If he is alive, he may reform yet and be like his father to you, his people, whom he has caused to suffer so much."

These words touched the poor beast so deeply that he ceased to beat himself against the iron bars of the cage in which the hunters carried him about, and became gentle as a lamb. He let himself be taken quietly to a menagerie, where all sorts of strange and ferocious animals were kept—a place which he had often visited as a boy, but never thought he should be shut up there himself.

However, he knew he deserved it all, and he began to apologize by showing himself very obedient to his keeper. This keeper was almost as great a brute as the animals he had charge of, and when he was in a bad mood he beat them without rhyme or reason. One day, while the keeper was sleeping, a tiger broke loose and leaped upon him, eager to devour him. Cherry at first felt a thrill of pleasure at the thought of revenge. Then, seeing how helpless the man was, he longed to be free so that he could defend him. Immediately the doors of his cage opened. The keeper, waking up, saw the strange beast leap out and imagined, of course, that he was going to be killed at once. Instead, he saw the tiger lying dead, and the strange beast creeping up and laying itself at his feet to be caressed. But as he lifted up his hand to stroke it, a voice said, "Good actions never go unrewarded." Instead of the frightful monster, there crouched on the ground nothing but a pretty little dog.

Cherry, delighted to find himself thus changed, caressed the keeper until at last the man took him up into his arms and carried him to the king. He told this wonderful story, from beginning to end. The queen wished to have the charming little dog, and Cherry would have been extremely happy if he could have forgotten that he was originally a man and a king. He was lodged most elegantly, had the richest of collars to adorn his neck, and heard himself praised continually. But his beauty brought him into trouble, for the queen, afraid lest he might grow too large for a pet, took advice of dog doctors. They ordered that he should be fed entirely upon bread, and that very sparingly; so poor Cherry was sometimes nearly starved.

One day, when they gave him his crust for breakfast, an idea seized him to go and eat it in the palace garden. He took the bread in his mouth and trotted away toward a stream which he knew, and where he sometimes stopped to drink. But instead of the stream he saw a splendid palace, glittering with gold and precious stones. Entering the doors was a crowd of men and women, magnificently dressed. Within there was singing and dancing and good cheer of all sorts. Yet, however grandly and merrily the people went in, Cherry noticed that those who came out were pale, thin, ragged, half-naked, covered with wounds and sores. Some of them dropped dead at once. Others dragged themselves on a little way and then lay down, dying of hunger, and vainly begged a morsel of bread from others who were entering in—who never took the least notice of them.

Cherry noticed one woman, who was trying feebly to gather and eat some green herbs. "Poor thing!" he said to himself. "I know what it is to be hungry, and I want my breakfast badly enough; but it will not kill me to wait until dinnertime, and my crust may save the life of this poor woman."

The little dog ran up to her and dropped his bread at her feet. She picked it up and ate it eagerly. Soon she looked quite recovered, and a delighted Cherry trotted back again to his kennel. On his way, he heard loud cries and saw a young girl dragged by four men to the door of the palace, which they were trying to force her to enter. The young girl was no other than his beloved Zelia. Oh, how he wished himself a monster again, as when he slew the tiger! Alas! What could a poor little dog do to defend her? But he ran forward and barked at the men, and bit their heels, until at last they chased him away with heavy blows. And then he lay down outside the palace door, determined to watch and see what had become of Zelia.

Conscience pricked him now. *I am furious against these wicked men, who are carrying her away; and did I not do the same myself?* he thought. *Did I not cast her into prison, and intend to sell her as a slave? Who knows how much more wickedness I might have done to her and others, if Heaven's justice had not stopped me in time.*

While he lay thinking and repenting, he heard a window open and saw Zelia throw out of it a bit of dainty meat. Cherry was just about to eat it when the woman to whom he had given his crust snatched him up in her arms.

"Poor little beast!" she cried, patting him. "Every bit of food in that palace is poisoned. You shall not touch a morsel."

At the same time the voice in the air repeated again, "Good actions never go unrewarded," and Cherry found himself changed into a beautiful little white pigeon. He remembered with joy that white was the color of the fairy Candide, and he began to hope that she was taking him into favor again.

He stretched his wings, delighted that he might now have a chance of approaching his fair Zelia. He flew up to the palace windows, and, finding one of them open, entered and looked everywhere, but he could not find Zelia. Then, in despair, he flew out again, determined to go over the world until he saw her once more.

He took flight at once and crossed many countries, swiftly as a bird can, but he found no trace of his beloved. After a long while in a desert, he sat beside an old hermit just outside his cave and shared his frugal meal. In the cave, Cherry saw a poor peasant girl—Zelia! Transported with joy, he flew in, perched on her shoulder, and expressed his delight and affection.

She was charmed by the pretty little pigeon and caressed it in return. She promised that if it would stay with her she would love it always.

"What have you done, Zelia?" said the hermit, smiling; and while he spoke the white pigeon vanished, and there stood Prince Cherry in his own natural form. "Your enchantment ended, Prince, when Zelia promised to love you. Indeed, she has loved you always, but your many faults forced her to hide her love. These are now amended, and you may both live happy if you will, because your union is built upon mutual respect and admiration."

Cherry and Zelia threw themselves at the feet of the hermit, whose form also began to change. His soiled garments became of dazzling whiteness, and his long beard and withered face grew into the flowing hair and lovely countenance of the fairy Candide.

"Rise up, my children," she said. "I must now transport you to your palace and restore to Prince Cherry his father's crown, of which he is now worthy."

She had scarcely ceased speaking when they found themselves in the chamber of Suliman. The old man was delighted to find again his beloved pupil and master, willingly gave up the throne, and became the most faithful of his subjects.

King Cherry and Queen Zelia reigned together for many years, and it is said that the king was so blameless and strict in all his duties that though he constantly wore the ring which Candide had given back to him, it never once pricked his finger enough to make it bleed.

PART TWO

Magical Wishes

"There's no use trying," she said: "one can't believe impossible things."

"I daresay you haven't had much practice," said the Queen. "When I was your age, I always did it for half-an-hour a day. Why, sometimes I've believed as many as six impossible things before breakfast."

—**Lewis Carroll,** *Through the Looking-Glass*

FOUR

Kenneth and the Carp

by Edith Nesbit

from *The Magic World* (1912)

Kenneth's cousins had often stayed with him, but he had never until now stayed with them. And you know how different everything is when you are in your own house. You are certain exactly what games the grown-ups dislike and what games they will not notice; also what sort of mischief is looked over and what sort is not. And, being accustomed to your own sort of grown-ups, you can always be pretty sure when you are likely to catch it. Whereas strange houses are, in this matter of catching it, full of the most unpleasing surprises.

Kenneth did not know what were the sort of things which, in his cousins' house, led to disapproval, punishment, scoldings; in short, to catching it. So the business of cousin Ethel's jewel-case, which is where this story ought to begin, was really not Kenneth's fault at all. Though for a time. . . . But I am getting on too fast.

Kenneth's cousins were four—Conrad, Alison, George, and Ethel. The first three were near his age, but Ethel was hardly like a cousin at all, more like an aunt, because she was grown up. She wore long dresses and all her hair on the top of her head, a mass of combs and hairpins; in fact she had just had her twenty-first birthday with iced cakes and a party and lots of presents, most of them jewelry. And that brings me again to the jewel-case, or would bring me if I were not determined to tell things in their proper order, which is the first duty of a storyteller.

Kenneth's home was in Kent, a wooden house among cherry orchards, and the nearest river five miles away. That was why he looked forward in such an excited way to visiting his cousins. Their house was very old, red brick with ivy all over it. It had a secret staircase, only the secret was not kept any longer, and the housemaids carried pails and brooms up and down the staircase. And the house was surrounded by a deep moat, with clear water in it, and long weeds and water lilies and fish—gold and silver and everyday kinds.

The first evening of Kenneth's visit passed uneventfully. His bedroom window looked over the moat, and early next morning he tried to catch fish with several pieces of string

knotted together and a hairpin kindly lent to him by the par-
lor maid. He did not catch any fish, partly because he baited
the hairpin with brown soap, and it washed off.

"Besides, fish hate soap," Conrad told him, "and that hook
of yours would do for a whale perhaps. Only we don't stock
our moat with whales. I'll ask Father to lend you his rod; it's
a spiffing one, much jollier than ours. And I won't tell the
kids because they'd never let it down on you. Fishing with a
hairpin!"

"Thank you very much," said Kenneth, feeling that his
cousin was a man and a brother. The kids were only two or
three years younger than he, but that is a great deal when
you are the elder; and besides, one of the kids was a girl.

"Alison's a bit of a sneak," Conrad used to say when anger
overcame politeness and brotherly feeling. Afterwards, when
the anger was gone and the other things left, he would say,
"You see she went to a beastly school for a bit, at Brighton,
for her health. And Father says they must have bullied her.
All girls are not like it, I believe."

But her sneakish qualities, if they really existed, were generally hidden, and she was very clever at thinking of new
games, and very kind if you got into a quarrel over anything.

George was eight and stout. He was not a sneak. He never
could keep a secret unless he forgot it. Which fortunately
happened quite often.

The uncle cheerfully loaned Kenneth his fishing rod and

provided real bait in the most generous manner. The four children fished all morning and all afternoon. Conrad caught two silver-white fish and an eel. Nothing was what the other three caught. But it was glorious sport. And the next day there was to be a picnic. Life to Kenneth seemed full of new and delicious excitement.

In the evening Kenneth's aunt and uncle went out to dinner, and Ethel, in her grown-up way, went with them, very grand in a blue silk dress and turquoises. So the children were left to themselves.

You know the empty hush which settles down on a house when the grown-ups have gone out to dinner and you have the whole evening to do what you like. The children stood in the hall a moment after the carriage wheels had died away with the scrunching swish that the carriage wheels always made as they turned the corner by the lodge, where the gravel was extra thick and soft owing to the droppings from the trees. From the kitchen came the voices of the servants, laughing and talking.

"It's two hours at least to bedtime," said Alison. "What shall we do?" Alison always began by saying "What shall we do?" and always ended by deciding what should be done.

"You all say what you think," she went on, "and then we'll vote about it. You first, Ken, because you're the visitor."

"Fishing," said Kenneth, because it was the only thing he could think of.

"Make toffee," said Conrad.

"Build a great big house with all the bricks," said George.

"We can't make toffee," Alison explained gently but firmly, "because you know what the pan was like last time, and Cook said, 'never again.' And it's no good building houses, Georgie, when you could be out of doors. And fishing's simply rotten when we've been at it all day. I've thought of something."

So of course all the others said, "What?"

"We'll have a river pageant on the moat. We'll all dress up and hang Chinese lanterns in the trees. I'll be the Sun-flower lady that the Troubadour came all across the sea for, because he loved her so, and one of you can be the Trouba-dour, and the others can be sailors or anything you like."

"I shall be the Troubadour," said Conrad with decision.

"I think you ought to let Kenneth because he's the visi-tor," said George, who did not see why Conrad should be a troubadour if *he* couldn't.

Conrad said what manners required, which was, "Oh! all right, I don't care about being the beastly Troubadour."

"You might be the Princess's brother," Alison suggested.

"Not me," said Conrad scornfully. "I'll be the captain of the ship."

"In a turban the brother would be, with the cloak from India, and the Persian dagger out of the cabinet in the draw-ing room," Alison went on.

"I'll be that," said George.

"No, you won't, I shall, so there," said Conrad. "You can be the captain of the ship."

(But in the end both boys were captains, because that meant being on the boat, whereas being the Princess's brother, however turbaned, only meant standing on the bank. And there is no rule to prevent captains wearing turbans and Persian daggers, except in the Navy where, of course, it is not done.)

So then they all tore up to the attic where the dressing-up trunk was, and pulled out all the dressing-up things on to the floor. And all the time they were dressing, Alison was telling the others what they were to say and do. The Princess wore a white satin skirt and a red flannel blouse and a veil formed of several motor scarves of various colors. Also a wreath of pink roses off one of Ethel's old hats, and a pair of pink satin slippers with sparkly buckles.

Kenneth wore a blue silk dressing jacket and a yellow sash, a lace collar, and a towel turban. And the others divided between them an eastern dressing gown, once the property of their grandfather, a black spangled scarf, very holey, a pair of red and white football stockings, a Chinese coat, and two old muslin curtains, which, rolled up, made turbans of enormous size and fierceness.

On the landing outside cousin Ethel's open door Alison paused and said, "I say!"

"Oh! come on," said Conrad, "we haven't fixed the Chinese lanterns yet, and it's getting dark."

"You go on," said Alison. "I've just thought of something."

The children were allowed to play in the boat so long as they didn't untie it from its moorings. The rope used to tie up the boat was extremely long, and gave the effect of coming home from a long voyage when the three boys pushed the boat out as far as it would go among the branches of the beech tree, which overhung the water, and then reappeared in the circle of red and yellow light thrown by the Chinese lanterns.

"What ho! Ashore there!" shouted the captain.

"What ho!" said Alison's disguised voice from the shore.

"We be three poor mariners," said Conrad, "just newly come to shore. We seek news of the Princess of Tripoli."

"She's in her palace," said the disguised voice. "Wait a minute, and I'll tell her you're here. But what do you want her for?"

"A poor minstrel of France," said Conrad, "who has heard of the Princess's beauty has come to lay, to lay—"

"His heart," said Alison.

"All right, I know. His heart at her something-or-other feet."

"Pretty feet," said Alison. "I go to tell the Princess."

Next moment from the shadows on the bank a radiant vision stepped into the circle of light, crying, "Oh! Rudel, is it indeed thou? Thou art come at last. Oh, welcome to the arms of the Princess!"

"What do I do now?" whispered Rudel (who was Kenneth) in the boat.

At the same moment Conrad and George said, as with one voice, "Alison, won't you catch it!"

At the end of the Princess's speech she had thrown back her veils and revealed a blaze of splendor. She wore several necklaces, one of seed pearls, one of topazes, and one of Australian shells, besides a string of amber and one of coral. And the front of the red flannel blouse was studded with brooches, in one at least of which diamonds gleamed. Each arm had one or two bracelets and on her clenched hands glittered as many rings as any Princess could wish to wear.

So her brothers had some excuse for saying, "You'll catch it."

"No, I shan't. It's my business, anyhow. Do shut up," said the Princess, stamping her foot. "Now then, Ken, go ahead. Ken, you say, 'Oh Lady, I faint with rapture!' "

"I faint with rapture," said Kenneth stolidly. "Now I land, don't I?"

He landed and stared at the jeweled hand the Princess held out.

"At last, at last," she said, "but you ought to say that, Ken. I say, I think I'd better be an eloping Princess, and then I can come in the boat. Rudel dies really, but that's so dull. Lead me to your ship, oh, noble stranger! For you have won the

Princess, and with you I will live and die. Give me your hand, can't you, silly, and do watch out for my dress train."

So Kenneth led her to the boat, and with some difficulty, for the satin train got between her feet, she managed to struggle into the boat.

"Now you stand and bow," she said. "Fair Rudel, with this ring I thee wed," she pressed a large amethyst ring into his hand. "Remember that the Princess of Tripoli is yours forever. Now let's sing *Integer Vitae* because it's Latin."

So they sat in the boat and sang. And presently the servants came out to listen and admire, and at the sound of the servants' approach the Princess veiled her shining splendor.

"It's prettier than wot the Coventry pageant was, so it is," said the cook, "but it's long past your bedtimes. So come on out of that there dangerous boat, there's dears."

So then the children went to bed. And when the house was quiet again, Alison slipped down and put back Ethel's jewelry, fitting the things into their cases and boxes as correctly as she could. *Ethel won't notice*, she thought, but of course Ethel did.

The next day each child was asked separately by Ethel's mother who had been playing with Ethel's jewelry. And Conrad and George said they would rather not say. This was an answer they always used in that family when that sort of question was asked, and it meant, "It wasn't me, and I don't want to snitch."

And when it came to Alison's turn, she found to her surprise and horror that instead of saying, "I played with them," she had said, "I would rather not say."

Of course, the mother thought that it was Kenneth who had had the jewels to play with. So when it came to his turn he was not asked the same question as the others, but his aunt said, "Kenneth, you are a very naughty little boy to take your cousin Ethel's jewelry to play with."

"I didn't," said Kenneth.

"Hush! hush!" said the aunt. "Do not make your fault worse by untruthfulness. And what have you done with the amethyst ring?"

Kenneth was just going to say that he had given it back to Alison, when he saw that this would be sneakish. So he said, getting hot to the ears, "You don't suppose I've stolen your beastly ring, do you, Auntie?"

"Don't you dare to speak to me like that," the aunt very naturally replied. "No, Kenneth, I do not think you would steal, but the ring is missing and it must be found."

Kenneth was furious and frightened. He stood looking down and kicking the leg of the chair.

"You had better look for it. You will have plenty of time, because I shall not allow you to go to the picnic with the others. The mere taking of the jewelry was wrong, but if you had owned your fault and asked Ethel's pardon, I should have overlooked it. But you have told me an untruth and you have lost the ring. You are a very wicked child, and it will make your dear mother very unhappy when she hears of it. That her boy should be a liar. It is worse than being a thief!"

At this Kenneth's courage gave way, and he lost his head. "Oh, don't," he said. "I didn't. I didn't. I didn't. Oh! Don't tell Mother I'm a thief and a liar. Oh! Aunt Effie, please, *please* don't." And with that he began to cry.

Any doubts Aunt Effie might have had were settled by this outbreak. It was now quite plain to her that Kenneth had really intended to keep the ring.

"You will remain in your room till the picnic party has started," the aunt went on, "and then you must find the ring. Remember I expect it to be found when I return. And I hope you will be in a better frame of mind and really sorry for having been so wicked."

"Mayn't I see Alison?" was all he found to say.

And the answer was, "Certainly not. I cannot allow you to associate with your cousins. You are not fit to be with honest, truthful children."

So they all went to the picnic, and Kenneth was left alone. When they had gone he crept down and wandered furtively through the empty rooms, ashamed to face the servants, and feeling almost as wicked as though he had really done something wrong. He thought about it all, over and over again, and the more he thought the more certain he was that he *had* handed back the ring to Alison last night when the voices of the servants were first heard from the dark lawn.

But what was the use of saying so? No one would believe him, and it would be snitching anyhow. Besides, perhaps he *hadn't* handed it back to her. Or rather, perhaps he had handed it and she hadn't taken it. Perhaps it had slipped into the boat. He would go and see.

But he did not find it in the boat, though he turned up the carpet and even took up the boards to look. And then an extremely miserable little boy began to search for an amethyst ring in all sorts of impossible places, indoors and out.

The servants gave him his meals and told him to cheer up. But cheering up and Kenneth were, for the time, strangers. Cook was sorry for Kenneth and sent him up a very nice dinner and a very nice tea. Roast chicken and gooseberry pie the dinner was, and for tea there was cake with almond icing on it.

The sun was very low when he went back wearily to have one more look in the boat for that detestable amethyst ring. Of course, it was not there. And the picnic party would be home soon. And he really did not know what his aunt would do to him.

"Shut me up in a dark cupboard, perhaps," he thought gloomily, "or put me to bed all day tomorrow. Or give me lines to write out, thousands, and thousands, and thousands, and thousands, and thousands of them."

The boat, set in motion by his stepping into it, swung out to the full length of its rope. The sun was shining almost level across the water. It was a very still evening, and the reflections of the trees and of the house were as distinct as the house and the trees themselves. And the water was unusually clear. He could see the fish swimming about, and the sand and pebbles at the bottom of the moat. How clear and quiet it looked down there, and what fun the fishes seemed to be having.

"I wish I was a fish," said Kenneth. "Nobody punishes *them* for taking rings they *didn't* take."

And then suddenly he saw the ring itself, lying calm, and quiet, and round, and shining, on the smooth sand at the bottom of the moat.

He reached for the boat hook and leaned over the edge of the boat trying to get up the ring on the boat hook's point. Then there was a splash.

"Good gracious! I wonder what that is?" said Cook in the kitchen, and dropped the saucepan with the Welsh rabbit in it which she had just made for kitchen supper.

Kenneth had leaned out too far over the edge of the boat, the boat had suddenly decided to go the other way, and Kenneth had fallen into the water.

The first thing he felt was delicious coolness, the second that his clothes had gone, and the next thing he noticed was that he was swimming quite easily and comfortably under water, and that he had no trouble with his breathing, such as people who tell you not to fall into water seem to expect you to have. Also he could see quite well, which he had never been able to do under water before.

I can't think, he said to himself, *why people make so much fuss about your falling into the water. I shan't be in a hurry to get out. I'll swim right round the moat while I'm about it.*

It was a much longer swim than he expected, and as he swam he noticed one or two things that struck him as rather odd. One was that he couldn't see his hands. And another was that he couldn't feel his feet. And he met some enormous fishes, like great cod or halibut, they seemed. He had had no idea that there were freshwater fish of that size.

They towered above him more like men-o'war than fish, and he was rather glad to get past them. There were numbers of smaller fishes, some about his own size, he thought. They seemed to be enjoying themselves extremely, and he admired the clever quickness with which they darted out of the way of the great hulking fish.

And then suddenly he ran into something hard and very solid, and a voice above him said crossly, "Now then, who are you a-shoving? Can't you keep your eyes open, and keep your nose out of gentlemen's shirt fronts?"

"I beg your pardon," said Kenneth, trying to rub his nose, and not being able to. "I didn't know people could talk under water," he added very much astonished to find that talking under water was as easy to him as swimming there.

"Fish can talk under water, of course," said the voice. "If they didn't, they'd never talk at all: they certainly can't talk out of it."

"But I'm not a fish," said Kenneth, and felt himself grin at the absurd idea.

"Yes, you are," said the voice. "Of course, you're a fish," and Kenneth, with a shiver of certainty, felt that the voice spoke the truth. He was a fish. He must have become a fish at the very moment when he fell into the water. That accounted for his not being able to see his hands or feel his feet. Because of course his hands were fins and his feet were a tail.

"Who are you?" he asked the voice, and his own voice trembled.

"I'm the Doyen Carp," said the voice. "You must be a very new fish indeed or you'd know that. Come up, and let's have a look at you."

Kenneth came up and found himself face to face with an enormous fish who had round staring eyes and a mouth that opened and shut continually. It opened square like a kit-bag, and it shut with an extremely sour and severe expression like that of an offended rhinoceros.

"Yes," said the Carp, "you *are* a new fish. Who put you in?"

"I fell in," said Kenneth, "out of the boat, but I'm not a fish at all, really I'm not. I'm a boy, but I don't suppose you'll believe me."

"Why shouldn't I believe you?" asked the Carp, wagging a slow fin. "Nobody tells untruths under water."

And if you come to think of it, no one ever does.

"Tell me your true story," said the Carp very lazily. And Kenneth told it.

"Ah! these humans!" said the Carp when he had done. "Always in such a hurry to think the worst of everybody!" He opened his mouth squarely and shut it contemptuously. "You're jolly lucky, you are. Not one boy in a million turns into a fish, let me tell you."

"Do you mean that I've got to *go on* being a fish?" Kenneth asked.

"Of course, you'll go on being a fish as long as you stop in the water. You couldn't live here, you know, if you weren't."

"I might if I was an eel," said Kenneth, and thought himself very clever.

"Well, *be* an eel then," said the Carp, and swam away, sneering and stately. Kenneth had to swim his hardest to catch up.

"Then if I get out of the water, shall I be a boy again?" he asked, panting.

"Of course, silly," said the Carp, "only you can't get out."

"Oh! can't I?" said Kenneth the fish, whisked his tail and swam off. He went straight back to the amethyst ring, picked it up in his mouth, and swam into the shallows at the edge of the moat. Then he tried to climb up the slanting mud and on to the grassy bank, but the grass hurt his fins horribly, and when he put his nose out of the water, the air stifled him, and he was glad to slip back again. Then he tried to jump out of the water, but he could only jump straight up into the air, so of course he fell straight down again into the water. He began to be afraid, and the thought that perhaps he was doomed to remain forever a fish was indeed a terrible one. He wanted to cry, but the tears would not come out of his eyes. Perhaps there was no room for any more water in the moat.

The smaller fishes called to him in a friendly way to come and play with them. They were having a quite exciting game of follow-the-leader among some enormous water lily stalks that looked like trunks of great trees. But Kenneth had no heart for games just then.

He swam miserably round the moat looking for the old Carp, his only acquaintance in this strange wet world. And at last, pushing through a thick tangle of water weeds he found the great fish.

"Now then," said the Carp testily, "haven't you any better manners than to come tearing a gentleman's bed-curtains like that?"

"I beg your pardon," said Kenneth Fish, "but I know how clever you are. Do please help me."

"What do you want now?" said the Carp, and spoke a little less crossly.

"I want to get out. I want to go and be a boy again."

"But you must have said you wanted to be a fish."

"I didn't mean it, if I did."

"You shouldn't say what you don't mean."

"I'll try not to again," said Kenneth humbly, "but how can I get out?"

"There's only one way," said the Carp, rolling his vast body over in his watery bed, "and a jolly unpleasant way it is. Far better stay here and be a good little fish. On the honor of a gentleman that's the best thing you can do."

"I want to get out," said Kenneth again.

"Well, then, the only way is . . . you know we always teach the young fish to look out for hooks so that they may avoid them. *You* must look out for a hook and *take* it. Let them catch you. On a hook."

The Carp shuddered and went on solemnly, "Have you strength? Have you patience? Have you high courage and determination? You will need them all. Have you all these?"

"I don't know what I've got," said poor Kenneth, "except that I've got a tail and fins, and I don't know a hook when I see it. Won't you come with me? Oh! dear Mr. Doyen Carp, *do* come and show me a hook."

"It will hurt you," said the Carp, "very much indeed. You take a gentleman's word for it."

"I know," said Kenneth. "You needn't rub it in."

The Carp rolled heavily out of his bed.

"Come on then," he said. "I don't admire your taste, but

if you want a hook, well, the gardener's boy is fishing in the cool of the evening. Come on."

He led the way with a steady stately movement.

"I want to take the ring with me," said Kenneth, "but I can't get hold of it. Do you think you could put it on my fin with your snout?"

"My what!" shouted the old Carp indignantly and stopped.

"Your nose, I meant," said Kenneth. "Oh! please don't be angry. It would be so kind of you if you would. Shove the ring on, I mean."

"That will hurt too," said the Carp, and Kenneth thought he seemed not altogether sorry that it should.

It did hurt very much indeed. The ring was hard and heavy, and somehow Kenneth's fin would not fold up small enough for the ring to slip over it, and the Carp's big mouth was rather clumsy at the work. But at last it was done. And then they set out in search of a hook for Kenneth to be caught with.

"I wish we could find one! I wish we could!" Kenneth Fish kept saying.

"You're just looking for trouble," said the Carp. "Well, here you are!"

Above them in the clear water hung a delicious-looking worm. Kenneth Boy did not like worms any better than you do, but to Kenneth Fish that worm looked most tempting and delightful.

"Just wait a sec," he said, "till I get that worm."

"You little silly," said the Carp. "*That's the hook.* Take it."

"Wait a sec," said Kenneth again.

His courage was beginning to ooze out of his fin tips, and a shiver ran down him from gills to tail.

"If you once begin to think about a hook you never take it," said the Carp.

"Never?" said Kenneth. "Then . . . oh! Goodbye!" he cried desperately, and snapped at the worm. A sharp pain ran through his head and he felt himself drawn up into the air, that stifling, choking, husky, thick stuff in which fish cannot breathe. And as he swung in the air the dreadful thought came to him, *Suppose I don't turn into a boy again? Suppose I keep being a fish?* And then he wished he hadn't. But it was too late to wish that.

Everything grew quite dark, only inside his head there seemed to be a light. There was a wild, rushing, buzzing noise, then something in his head seemed to break and he knew no more.

When presently he knew things again, he was lying on something hard. Was he Kenneth Fish lying on a stone at the bottom of the moat, or Kenneth Boy lying somewhere out of the water? His breathing was all right, so he wasn't a fish out of water or a boy under it.

"He's coming to," said a voice. The next moment he knew it to be the voice of his aunt, and he moved his hand and felt grass in it. He opened his eyes and saw above him the soft gray of the evening sky with a star or two.

"Here's the ring, Aunt," he said.

The cook had heard a splash and had run out just as the picnic party arrived at the front door. They had all rushed to the moat, and the uncle had pulled Kenneth out with the boat hook. He had not been in the water more than three minutes, they said. But Kenneth knew better.

They carried him in, very wet he was, and laid him on the breakfast-room sofa, where the aunt with hurried thought-fulness had spread out the uncle's mackintosh.

"Get some rough towels, Jane," said the aunt. "And hurry!"

"I got the ring," said Kenneth.

"Never mind about the ring, dear," said the aunt, taking his boots off.

"But you said I was a thief and a liar," Kenneth said feebly, "and it was in the moat all the time."

"*Mother!*" it was Alison who shrieked. "You didn't say that to him?"

"Of course, I didn't," said the aunt impatiently. She thought she hadn't, but then Kenneth thought she had.

"It was *me* took the ring," said Alison, "and I dropped it. I didn't say I hadn't. I only said I'd rather not say. Oh, Mother! Poor Kenneth!"

The aunt, without a word, carried Kenneth up to the bathroom and turned on the hot water tap. The uncle and Ethel followed.

"Why didn't you own up, you sneak?" said Conrad to his sister with withering scorn.

"Sneak," echoed the stout George.

"I meant to. I was only getting steam up," sobbed Alison. "I didn't know. Mother only told us she wasn't pleased with Ken, and so he wasn't to go to the picnic. Oh! What shall I do? What shall I do?"

"Sneak!" said her brothers in chorus, and left her to her tears of shame and regret.

It was Kenneth who next day begged everyone to forgive and forget. And since it was *his* day—rather like a birthday, you know—when no one could refuse him anything, all agreed that the whole affair should be buried in forgetfulness. Everyone was tremendously kind, the aunt more so than anyone. But Alison's eyes were still red when in the afternoon they all went fishing once more. And before Kenneth's hook had been two minutes in the water there was a bite, a very big fish. The uncle had to be called from his study to land it.

"Here's a magnificent fellow," said the uncle. "Not an ounce less than two pounds, Ken. I'll have it stuffed for you."

And he held out the fish and Kenneth found himself face to face with the Doyen Carp.

There was no mistaking that mouth that opened like a

kit-bag, and shut in a sneer like a rhinoceros's. Its eye was most reproachful.

"Oh, no!" cried Kenneth. "You helped me back and I'll help you back," and he caught the Carp from the hands of the uncle and flung it out in the moat.

"Your head's not quite right yet, my boy," said the uncle kindly. "Hadn't you better go in and lie down a bit?"

But Alison understood, for he had told her the whole story. He had told her that morning before breakfast while she was still in deep disgrace, to cheer her up, he said. And, most disappointingly, it made her cry more than ever.

"Your poor little fins," she had said, "and having your feet tied up in your tail. And it was all my fault."

"I liked it," Kenneth had said. "It was a most awful lark." And he quite meant what he said.

FIVE

The Skipping Shoes

by Louisa May Alcott

from *Lulu's Library*, Vol. 1, *A Christmas Dream* (1886)

Once there was a little girl, named Kitty, who never wanted to do what people asked her. She said "I won't" and "I can't," and did not run at once pleasantly, as helpful children do.

One day her mother gave her a pair of new shoes; and after a fuss about putting them on, Kitty said, as she lay kicking on the floor, "I wish these were seven-leagued boots, like Jack the Giant Killer's; then it would be easy to run errands all the time. Now, I hate to keep trotting, and I don't like new shoes, and I won't stir a step."

Just as she said that, the shoes gave a skip, and set her on her feet so suddenly that it scared all the naughtiness out of her. She stood looking at these curious shoes, and the bright buttons on them seemed to wink at her like eyes, while the heels tapped on the floor a sort of tune. Before she dared to stir, her mother called from the next room, "Kitty, run and tell the cook to make a pie for dinner; I forgot it."

"I don't want to," began Kitty, with a whine as usual.

But the words were hardly out of her mouth when the shoes gave one jump, and took her downstairs, through the hall, and landed her at the kitchen door. Her breath was nearly gone, but she gave the message, and turned round, trying to see if the shoes would let her walk at all. They went nicely until she wanted to turn into the china closet where the cake was. She was forbidden to touch it, but loved to fake a bit when she could. Now she found that her feet were fixed fast to the floor, and could not be moved until her father said, as he passed the window close by, "You will have time to go to the post office before school and get my letters."

"I can't," began Kitty, but away went the shoes, out of the house at one bound, and trotted down the street so fast that the maid who ran after her with her hat could not catch her.

"I can't stop!" cried Kitty, and she did not until the shoes took her straight into the post office.

"What's the hurry today?" asked the man, as he saw her without any hat, all rosy and breathless, and her face puckered up as if she did not know whether to laugh or to cry.

I won't tell anyone about these dreadful shoes, and I'll take them off as soon as I get home. I hope they will go back slowly, or people will think I'm crazy, thought Kitty, as she took the letters and went away.

The shoes walked nicely along until she came to the bridge. There she wanted to stop and watch some boys in a boat, forgetting school and her father's letters. But the shoes wouldn't stop, though she tried to make them, and held on to the railing as hard as she could. Her feet went on, and when she sat down, they still dragged her along so steadily that she had to go, and she got up feeling that there was something very strange about these shoes. The minute she gave up, all went smoothly, and she got home in good time.

"I won't wear these horrid things another minute," said Kitty, sitting on the doorstep and trying to unbutton the shoes.

But not a button could she move, though she got red and angry struggling to do it.

"Time for school; run away, little girl," called Mamma from upstairs, as the clock struck nine.

"I won't!" said Kitty, crossly.

But she did; for those magic shoes danced her off and landed her at her desk in five minutes.

Well, I'm not late; that's one comfort, she thought, wishing she had come pleasantly, and not been whisked away without any lunch.

Her legs were so tired with the long skips that she was glad to sit still; and that pleased the teacher, for generally Kitty was fussing about all lesson time. But at recess she got into trouble again when one of the children knocked down the house of corncobs she had built, and made her angry.

"Now, I'll kick yours down, and see how you like it, Dolly."

Up went her foot, but it didn't come down; it stayed in the air, and there she stood looking as if she were going to dance. The children laughed to see her, and she could do nothing till she said to Dolly in a great hurry, "Never mind; if you didn't mean to, I'll forgive you."

Then the foot went down, and Kitty felt so glad about it that she tried to be pleasant, fearing some new caper of those dreadful shoes. She began to understand how they worked, and thought she would see if she had any power over them. So, when one of the children wanted his ball, which had bounced over the hedge, she said kindly, "Perhaps I can get it for you, Willy."

And over she jumped as lightly as if she too were an India-rubber ball.

"How could you do it!" cried the boys, much surprised since not one of them dared try such a high leap.

Kitty laughed, and began to dance, feeling pleased and proud to find there was a good side to the shoes after all. Such twirlings and skippings as she made, such pretty steps and airy little bounds it was pretty to see; for it seemed as if her feet were bewitched, and went of themselves. The little girls were charmed, and tried to imitate her; but no one could, and they stood in a circle watching her dance until the bell rang. Then all rushed in to tell about it.

Kitty said it was her new shoes, and never told how strangely they acted, hoping to have good times now. But she was mistaken.

On the way home she wanted to stop and see her friend Belle's new doll. But at the gate her feet stuck fast, and she had to give up her wishes and go straight on, as Mamma had told her always to do.

"Run and pick a nice little dish of strawberries for dinner," said her sister, as she went in.

"I'm too ti—" There was no time to finish, for the shoes landed her in the middle of the strawberry bed at one jump.

"I might as well be a grasshopper if I'm to skip round like this," she said, forgetting to feel tired out there in the pleasant garden, with the robins picking berries close by, and a cool wind lifting the leaves to show where the reddest and ripest ones hid.

The little dish was soon filled, and she wanted to stay and eat a few, warm and sweet from the vines; but the bell rang, and away she went, over the wood-pile, across the piazza, and into the dining room before the berry in her mouth was half eaten.

"How this child does rush about today!" said her mother. "It is so delightful to have such a quick little errand girl that

I shall get her to carry some bundles to my poor people this afternoon."

"Oh, dear me! I do hate to lug those old clothes and bottles and baskets of cold food around. Must I do it?" sighed Kitty, while the shoes tapped on the floor under the table, as if to remind her that she must, whether she liked it or not.

"It would be right and kind, and would please me very much. But you may do as you choose about it. I am very tired, and someone must go. The little Bryan baby is sick and needs what I send," said Mamma, looking disappointed.

Kitty sat very still and sober for some time, and no one spoke to her. She was making up her mind whether she would go pleasantly or be whisked about like a grasshopper against her will. When dinner was over, she said in a cheerful voice, "I'll go, Mamma; and when all the errands are done, may I come back through Fairyland, as we call the little grove where the tall ferns grow?"

"Yes, dear; when you please me, I am happy to please you."

I'm glad I decided to be good. Now I shall have a lovely time, thought Kitty, as she trotted away with a basket in one hand, a bundle in the other, and some money in her pocket for a poor old woman who needed help.

The shoes went quietly along, and seemed to know just where to stop. The sick baby's mother thanked her for the soft little nightgowns. The lame girl smiled when she saw the books. The hungry children gathered round the basket of food, like young birds eager to be fed. And the old woman gave her a beautiful pink shell that her sailor son brought home from sea.

When all the errands were done, Kitty skipped away to Fairyland, feeling very happy, as people always do when they have done kind things. It was a lovely place; for the ferns made green arches tall enough for little girls to sit under, and the ground was covered with pretty green moss and wood flowers. Birds flew about in the pines, squirrels chattered in the oaks, butterflies floated here and there, and from the pond nearby came the croak of frogs sunning their green backs on the mossy stones.

"I wonder if the shoes will let me stop and rest; it is so cool here, and I'm so tired," said Kitty, as she came to a cozy nook at the foot of a tree.

The words were hardly out of her mouth when her feet folded under her, and there she sat on a cushion of moss, like the queen of the wood on her throne. Something lighted with a bump close by her, and looking down she saw a large black cricket with a stiff tail, staring at her curiously.

"Bless my heart! I thought you were some relation of my cousin Grasshopper's. You came down the hill with long leaps just like him; so I stopped to say, How d' ye do," said the cricket in its creaky voice.

"I'm not a grasshopper; but I have on fairy shoes today, and so I do many things that I never did before," answered

Kitty, much surprised to be able to understand what the cricket said.

"It is midsummer day, and fairies can play whatever pranks they like. If you didn't have those shoes on, you couldn't understand what I say. Listen, and hear those squirrels talk, and the birds, and the ants down here. Make the most of this chance; for at sunset your shoes will stop skipping, and the fun all be over."

While the cricket talked, Kitty did hear all sorts of little voices, singing, laughing, chatting in the merriest way, and understood every word they said. The squirrels called to one another as they raced:

> Here's a nut, there's a nut;
> Hide it quick away,
> In a hole, under leaves,
> To eat some winter day.
> Acorns sweet are plenty,
> We will have them all:
> Skip and scamper lively
> Till the last ones fall.

The birds were singing softly,

> Rock a bye, babies,
> Your cradle hangs high;
> Soft down your pillow,

Your curtain the sky.
Father will feed you,
While mother will sing,
And shelter our darlings
With her warm wing.

Ants were saying to one another as they hurried in and out of their little houses,

Work, neighbor, work!
Do not stop to play;
Wander far and wide,
Gather all you may.
We are never like
Idle butterflies,
But like the busy bees,
Industrious and wise.

"Ants always were dreadfully good, but butterflies are ever so much prettier," said Kitty, listening to the little voices with wonder and pleasure.

Hollo! hollo!
Come down below,
It's lovely and cool
Out here in the pool;
On a lily-pad float
For a nice green boat.

Here we sit and sing
In a pleasant ring;
Or leap-frog play,
In the jolliest way.
Our games have begun,
Come join in the fun.

"Dear me! What could I do over there in the mud with the green frogs?" laughed Kitty, as this song was croaked at her.

No, no, come and fly
Through the sunny sky,
Or honey sip
From the rose's lip,
Or dance in the air,
Like spirits fair.
Come away, come away;
'Tis our holiday.

A cloud of lovely yellow butterflies flew up from a wild-rose bush, and went dancing away higher and higher, till they vanished in the light beyond the wood.

"That is better than leap-frog. I wish my skipping shoes would let me fly up somewhere, instead of carrying me on errands and where I ought to go all the time," said Kitty, watching the pretty things glitter as they flew.

Just at that minute a clock struck, and away went the shoes

over the pool, the hill, the road, till they pranced in at the gate as the tea-bell rang. Kitty amused the family by telling what she had done and seen; but no one believed the Fairyland part, and her father said, laughing, "Go on, my dear, making up little stories, and by and by you may be as famous as Hans Christian Andersen, whose books you like so well."

The sun will soon set, and then my fun will be over; so I must skip while I can, thought Kitty, and went waltzing round the lawn so prettily that all the family came to see her.

"She dances so well that she shall go to dancing school," said her mother, pleased with the pretty antics of her little girl.

Kitty was delighted to hear that, for she had longed to go. She went on skipping as hard as she could, hoping she might learn some of the graceful steps the shoes took before the day was done.

"Come, dear, stop now, and run up to your bath and bed. It has been a long hot day, and you are tired; so get to sleep early, for Nurse wants to go out," said her mother, as the sun went down behind the hills with a last bright glimmer, like the wink of a great sleepy eye.

"Oh, please, a few minutes more," began Kitty, but was off like a flash; for the shoes trotted her upstairs so fast that she ran against old Nurse, and down she went, splashing the water all over the floor, and scolding in such a funny way that it made Kitty laugh so that she could hardly pick her up again.

By the time she was ready to undress the sun was quite gone, and the shoes she took off were common ones again, for midsummer day was over. But Kitty never forgot the little lessons she had learned. She tried to run willingly when spoken to. She remembered the pretty steps and danced like a fairy. And, best of all, she always loved the innocent and interesting little creatures in the woods and fields, and whenever she was told she might go to play with them, she hurried away almost as quickly as if she still wore the skipping shoes.

SIX

The Enchanted Necklace

by Annie Fellows Johnston

from *The Little Colonel's House Party* (1900)

Once upon a time, near a castle in a lonely wood, there lived an orphan maiden named Olga. She would have been all alone in the world had it not been for an old woman who befriended her. This woman was a flax-spinner and lived in a humble thatched cottage near the castle. She had taken pity on Olga when the little orphan was a helpless baby. So kind had she always been that Olga had grown up without feeling the lack of father, mother, brother, or sister. In all ways the old flax-spinner had taken their places.

Every morning Olga carried water from the spring, gathered the wild fruits of the woods, and spread the linen on the grass to bleach. This she did to help the old woman, for she had a good and grateful heart as well as a beautiful face.

One day as Olga was wandering by the spring, searching for watercress, the young prince of the castle rode by on his prancing charger. A snow-white plume waved in his hat, and a shining silver bugle hung from his shoulder, for he had been following the chase.

He was thirsty and tired, and asked for a drink, but there was no cup from which to dip the water from the spring. Olga caught the drops as they bubbled out from the spring, holding them in the hollow of her beautiful white hands, and, reaching up to where he sat, offered him the sparkling water. So gracefully was it done that the prince was charmed by her lovely face and modest manner. When he had satisfied his thirst, he touched her white hands with his lips. Before he rode away he asked her name and where she lived.

The next day a courier in scarlet and gold stopped at the door of the cottage and invited Olga to the castle. Princesses and royal ladies from all over the realm were to be entertained there, seven days and seven nights. Every night a grand ball would be given, and Olga was summoned to each of the balls. It was on account of her pleasing manner and her great beauty that she had been invited.

The old flax-spinner curtsied low to the royal messenger and promised that Olga should be at the castle without fail.

"But, good dame," cried Olga when the courier had gone,

"please tell me why you made such a promise, when you know full well this rough gown of flax is all I own? Would you have me stand before the prince in beggar's garb? Better to stay at home forever than be put to shame before such guests."

"Stop worrying, my child," the old dame said. "You shall wear a court robe of the finest. Years have I toiled to give it to you, but that is nothing. I loved you as my own."

Then the old woman went into an inner room and pricked herself with her spindle until a great red drop of her heart's blood fell into her trembling hand. With secret words she blew upon it, and rolled it in her palm, and turned and turned and turned it. As she turned and muttered, it shriveled into a tiny round ball like a seed. She strung it on to a thread with many others like it. Seventy times seven was the number of beads. Then she laid the necklace away until the time when it should be needed.

When the night of the first ball rolled around, Olga combed her long golden hair and twisted it with a wreath of snowy water-lilies. Then she stood before the old woman in her dress of tow. To her wonderment and grief she saw the old flax-spinner had no silken robe in waiting, only a string of beads which she fastened around Olga's white throat. Each bead in the necklace looked like a little shriveled seed, and Olga's eyes were filled with tears of disappointment.

"Obey me and all will be well," said the old dame. "When

you reach the castle gate, clasp one bead in your fingers and say:

For love's sweet sake, in my hour of need,
Blossom and deck me, little seed.

"Immediately, right royally shall you be dressed. You have been a good daughter to me, and thus I reward you. But remember carefully the charm. Only to the magic words, 'For love's sweet sake,' will the necklace give up its treasures. If you should forget, then you will be doomed always to wear your gown of tow."

Olga sped on her moon-lighted way through the forest until she came to the castle gate. There she paused, and grasping a bead of the strange necklace between her fingers, repeated the old woman's charm:

For love's sweet sake, in my hour of need,
Blossom and deck me, little seed.

Immediately the bead burst with a little puff, as if a seed-pod had snapped apart. A faint perfume surrounded her, rare and subtle as if it had been blown across from some flower of Eden. Olga looked down and found herself covered in a robe of such delicate texture that it seemed soft as a rose leaf, and as airy as the pink clouds that sometimes float across the sunset. The water-lilies in her hair had become a crown of opals.

When she entered the great ballroom, the prince of the

castle started up from his throne in amazement. Never before had he seen such a vision of loveliness. "Surely," he said, "some rose of Paradise has found a soul and drifted earthward to blossom here." All that night he had eyes for none but her.

The next night Olga started again to the castle in her dress of tow, and at the gate she grasped the second bead in her fingers, repeating the charm. This time the pale yellow of the daffodils seemed to have woven itself into a cloth of gold for her adorning. It was like a shimmer of moonbeams, and her hair held the diamond flashings of a hundred tiny stars.

That night the prince paid her so many compliments and singled her out so often to bestow his favors, Olga's head was turned. She tossed it proudly, and scorned the thought of the humble cottage which had given her shelter so long. The next day, when she had returned to her gown of tow and was no longer a haughty court lady but only Olga, the flax-spinner's maiden, she felt sorry for herself. Frowning, she carried the water from the spring. Frowning, she gathered the cresses and plucked the woodland fruit. And then she sat all day by the spring, refusing to spread the linen on the grass to bleach.

She was discontented with the old life of toil, and she pouted crossly because duties called her when she wanted to do nothing but sit idly dreaming of the court scenes in which she had taken a bright part. When the old flax-spinner saw Olga's frowns, her fingers trembled as she spun, for she had given of her heart's blood to buy happiness for the maiden she loved, and well she knew there can be no happiness where frowns abide. She felt that her years of sacrifice had been in vain.

That night outside the castle gate Olga paused. She had forgotten the charm. The day's discontent had darkened her memory as storm clouds darken the sky. But she grasped her necklace commandingly.

"Deck me at once!" she cried, in a haughty tone. "Clothe me more beautifully than mortal maid was ever clad before, so that I may find favor in the prince's sight and become the bride of the castle. I want to be done forever with the spindle and the distaff."

But the moon went under a cloud and the wind began to moan around the castle towers. The black night-hawks in the forests flapped their wings in warning, and the black bats flitted low around her head.

"Obey me at once!" she cried, angrily, stamping her foot and jerking at the necklace. But the string broke and the beads went rolling away in the darkness in every direction, and were lost. All but one, which she held clasped in her hand.

Then Olga wept at the castle gate; wept outside in the night and the darkness, in her beggar's dress of tow. But after awhile, through her sobbing, stole the answering sob of the night wind. "Hush-sh!" it seemed to say. "Sh-sh! Never a heart can come to harm, if the lips but speak the old dame's charm."

The voice of the night wind sounded so much like the

voice of the old flax-spinner that Olga was startled and looked around wonderingly. Then suddenly she seemed to see the little thatched cottage and the bent form of the lonely old woman at the wheel. All the years in which the good dame had befriended her seemed to rise up in a row, and out of each one called a thousand kindnesses as with one voice: "How can you forget us, Olga? We were done for you, for love's sweet sake and that alone."

Then Olga was sorry and ashamed that she had been so proud and forgetful, and she wept again. The tears seemed to clear her vision, for now she saw plainly that through no power of her own could she grasp favors from destiny. Only the power of the old charm could make them hers. She re-membered it then, and holding fast to the one bead in her hand, she repeated, humbly:

> For love's sweet sake, in my hour of need,
> Blossom and deck me, little seed.

As the words left her lips, the moon shone out from be-hind the clouds above the dark forest. There was a fragrance of lilies all about her, and a gossamer gown floated around her, whiter than the whiteness of the fairest lily. It was fine, like the finest lace that the frost-elves weave, and softer than the softest ermine of the snow. On her long golden hair gleamed a crown of pearls.

So beautiful, so dazzling was she as she entered the castle

door, that the prince came down to meet her, knelt and kissed her hand, and claimed her as his bride. Then came the bishop and led her to the throne, and before them all the flax-spinner's maiden was married to the prince, and made the Princess Olga.

Until the seven days and seven nights were done, the celebration lasted in the castle. In the merriment the old flax-spinner was again forgotten. Her kindness of the past, her loneliness in the present, had no part in the thoughts of the Princess Olga.

But the beads that had rolled away into the darkness buried themselves in the earth, and took root and sprang up. There at the castle gate they bloomed, a strange, strange flower, for on every stem hung a row of little bleeding hearts.

One day the Princess Olga, seeing them from her window, went down to them in wonderment. "What do you here?" she cried, for in her lonely forest life she had learned all speech of bird and beast and plant.

"We bloom for love's sweet sake," they answered. "We have sprung from the old flax-spinner's gift—the necklace you broke and scattered. From her heart's best blood she gave it, and her heart still bleeds to think she is forgotten."

Then they began to tell the story of the old woman's sacrifices, all the seventy times seven that she had given for the sake of the maiden. Olga grieved as she listened, that she could have been so ungrateful. Then she brought the prince to listen to the story of the strange flowers. When he had heard, together they went to the lowly cottage and fetched the old flax-spinner to the castle, there to live out all her days.

PART THREE

CLEVER HEROES

Great decisions often take no more than
a moment in the making.
—**Hugh Lofting,** *The Voyages of Doctor Dolittle*

SEVEN

The Gold-Bearded Man

by Andrew Lang

from *The Crimson Fairy Book* (1903)

Once upon a time there lived a great king who had a wife and one son whom he loved very much. The boy was still young when, one day, the king said to his wife, "I feel that the hour of my death draws near, and I want you to promise that you will never take another husband but will spend your life taking care of our son."

The queen burst into tears at these words, and sobbed out that she would never, never marry again, and that her son's welfare should be her first thought as long as she lived. Her promise comforted the troubled heart of the king, and after a few days he died, at peace with himself and with the world.

But no sooner was the breath out of his body, than the queen said to herself, "To promise is one thing, and to keep is quite another." Hardly was the last spadeful of earth flung over the coffin than she married a noble from a neighboring country, and got him made king instead of the young prince. Her new husband was a cruel, wicked man, who treated his stepson very badly, gave him scarcely anything to eat, and only rags to wear. He would have killed the boy if he hadn't feared the people.

By the palace grounds there ran a brook, but instead of being a water-brook it was a milk-brook. Both rich and poor flocked to it daily and drew as much milk as they chose. The first thing the new king did when he was seated on the throne was to forbid anyone to go near the brook. This was purely spite, for there was plenty of milk for everybody.

For some days no one dared go near the banks of the stream, but at last some of the watchmen noticed that early in the mornings, just at dawn, a man with a gold beard came down to the brook with a pail, which he filled up to the brim with milk. Then he vanished like smoke before they could get near enough to see who he was. So they went and told the king what they had seen.

At first the king would not believe their story, but as they insisted it was quite true, he said that he would go and watch the stream that night himself. With the earliest streaks of dawn the gold-bearded man appeared and filled his pail as before. Then in an instant he vanished, as if the earth had swallowed him up.

The king stood staring at the place where the man had disappeared. He had never seen him before, that was certain; but what mattered much more was how to catch him, and what should be done with him when he was caught? He would have a cage built as a prison for him, and everyone would talk of it. In other countries thieves were put in prison, and it had been a long time indeed since any king had used a cage.

It was all very well to plan, and even to station a watchman behind every bush, but it was of no use, for the man was never caught. They would creep up to him softly on the grass, as he was stooping to fill his pail, and just as they stretched out their hands to seize him, he vanished before their eyes. Time after time this happened, until the king grew mad with rage and offered a large reward to anyone who could tell him how to capture his enemy.

The first person that came with a scheme was an old soldier who promised the king that if he would only put some bread and bacon and a flask of wine on the bank of the stream, the gold-bearded man would be sure to eat and drink, and they could shake some powder into the wine, which would send him to sleep at once. After that there was nothing to do but to shut him in the cage.

This idea pleased the king, and he ordered bread and bacon and a flask of drugged wine to be placed on the bank of the stream, and the watchers to be redoubled. Then, full of hope, he awaited the result.

Everything turned out just as the soldier had said. Early next morning the gold-bearded man came down to the brook, ate, drank, and fell sound asleep, so that the watchers easily bound him, and carried him off to the palace. In a moment the king had him fast in the golden cage, and showed him to the strangers who were visiting his court. The poor captive, when he awoke from his drunken sleep, tried to talk to them, but no one would listen to him, so he shut himself up altogether, and the people who came to stare took him for a dumb man of the woods. He wept and moaned to himself all day and would hardly touch food. Fearing that he should die and escape his tormentors, the king ordered his chief cook to send the prisoner dishes from the royal table.

The gold-bearded man had been in captivity about a month when the king was forced to make war upon a neighboring country. He left the palace to take command of his army. But before he went he called his stepson to him and said, "Listen, boy, to what I tell you. While I am away I trust the care of my prisoner to you. See that he has plenty to eat and drink, but be careful that he does not escape, or even walk about the room. If I return and find him gone, you will pay for it by a terrible death."

The young prince was thankful that his stepfather was going to the war, and secretly hoped he might never come back. As soon as he had ridden off, the boy went to the room where the cage was kept and never left it night and day. He even played his games beside it.

One day he was shooting at a mark with a silver bow, and one of his arrows fell into the golden cage.

"Please give me my arrow," said the prince, running up to him.

The gold-bearded man answered, "No, I shall not give it to you unless you let me out of my cage."

"I may not let you out," replied the boy, "for if I do my stepfather says that I shall have to die a horrible death when he returns from the war. My arrow can be of no use to you, so give it to me."

The man handed the arrow through the bars, but when he had done so he begged harder than ever that the prince would open the door and set him free. Indeed, he prayed so earnestly that the prince's heart was touched, for he was a tenderhearted boy who pitied the sorrows of other people. So he shot back the bolt, and the gold-bearded man stepped out into the world.

"I will repay you a thousandfold for that good deed," said the man, and then he vanished. The prince began to think what he should say to the king when he came back; then he wondered whether it would be wise to wait for his stepfather's return and run the risk of the dreadful death which had been promised him. *No,* he thought, *I am afraid to stay. Perhaps the world will be kinder to me than he has been.*

Unseen, he stole out when twilight fell, and for many days he wandered over mountains and through forests and valleys without knowing where he was going or what he should do. He had only berries for food. Then one morning, he saw a wood pigeon sitting on a bough. In an instant he had fitted an arrow to his bow and was taking aim at the bird, thinking what a good meal he would make of him, when his weapon fell to the ground at the sound of the pigeon's voice, "Do not shoot, I implore you, noble prince! I have two little sons at home, and they will die of hunger if I am not there to bring them food."

The young prince had pity and unstrung his bow.

"Oh, prince, I will repay your deed of mercy," said the grateful wood pigeon.

"Poor thing! How can you repay me?" asked the prince.

"You have forgotten," answered the wood pigeon, "the proverb that says, 'Mountain and mountain can never meet, but one living creature can always come across another.' " The boy laughed at this speech and went his way.

By and by he reached the edge of a lake, and flying towards some rushes, which grew near the shore, he saw a wild duck. Now, in the days when the king, his father, had been alive, he had everything to eat he could possibly wish for. And the prince always had wild duck for his birthday dinner. So he quickly fitted an arrow to his bow and took a careful aim.

"Do not shoot, I pray you, noble prince!" cried the wild

duck. "I have two little sons at home; they will die of hunger if I am not there to bring them food."

And the prince had pity, and let fall his arrow and unstrung his bow.

"Oh, prince! I will repay your deed of mercy," exclaimed the grateful duck.

"You poor thing! How can you repay me?" asked the prince.

"You have forgotten," answered the duck, "the proverb that says, 'Mountain and mountain can never meet, but one living creature can always come across another.' " The boy laughed at this speech and went his way.

He had not wandered far from the shores of the lake, when he noticed a stork standing on one leg, and again he raised his bow and prepared to take aim.

"Do not shoot, I pray you, noble prince," cried the stork. "I have two little sons at home; they will die of hunger if I am not there to bring them food."

Again the prince was filled with pity, and this time also he did not shoot.

"Oh, prince, I will repay your deed of mercy," cried the stork.

"You poor stork! How can you repay me?" asked the prince.

"You have forgotten," answered the stork, "the proverb that says, 'Mountain and mountain can never meet, but one living creature can always come across another.' "

The boy laughed at hearing these words again, and walked

slowly on. He had not gone far, when he fell in with two discharged soldiers.

"Where are you going, little brother?" asked one.

"I am seeking work," answered the prince.

"So are we," replied the soldier. "We can all go together."

The boy was glad of company and they went on, and on, and on, through seven kingdoms, without finding anything they were able to do. At length they reached a palace, and there was the king standing on the steps.

"You seem to be looking for something," said he.

"It is work we want," they all answered.

So the king told the soldiers that they might become his coachmen, but he made the boy his companion and gave him rooms near his own. The soldiers were dreadfully angry when they heard this, for of course they did not know that the boy was really a prince. They soon began to put their heads together to plot his ruin.

Then they went to the king.

"Your Majesty," they said, "we think it our duty to tell you that your new companion has boasted to us that if he were only your steward he would not lose a single grain of corn out of the storehouses. Now, if your Majesty would give orders that a sack of wheat should be mixed with one of barley, and would send for the youth, and command him to separate the grains one from another, in two hours' time, you would soon see what his talk was worth."

The king, who was weak, listened to what these wicked men had told him, and desired the prince to have the contents of the sack piled into two heaps by the time that he returned from his council. "If you succeed," he added, "you shall be my steward, but if you fail, I will put you to death on the spot."

The unfortunate prince declared that he had never made any such boast as was reported, but it was all in vain. The king did not believe him. He put him into an empty room, told his servants to carry in the huge sack filled with wheat and barley, and scatter the grain in a heap on the floor.

The prince hardly knew where to begin, and if he had had a thousand people to help him, and a week to do it in, he could never have finished his task. So he flung himself on the ground in despair and covered his face with his hands.

While he lay thus, a wood pigeon flew in through the window.

"Why are you weeping, noble prince?" asked the wood pigeon.

"How can I help weeping at the task given to me by the king? For he says, if I fail to do it, I shall die a horrible death."

"Oh, there is really nothing to cry about," answered the wood pigeon soothingly. "I am the king of the wood pigeons, whose life you spared when you were hungry. And now I will repay my debt, as I promised." So saying he flew out of the window, leaving the prince with some hope in his heart.

In a few minutes he returned, followed by a cloud of wood

pigeons, so thick that it seemed to fill the room. Their king showed them what they had to do, and they set to work so hard that the grain was sorted into two heaps long before the council was over. When the king came back he could not believe his eyes. But search as he might through the two heaps, he could not find any barley among the wheat, or any wheat among the barley. So he praised the prince for his industry and cleverness, and made him his steward at once.

This made the two soldiers more envious still, and they began to hatch another plot.

"Your Majesty," they said to the king one day as he was standing on the steps of the palace, "that fellow has been boasting again, that if he had the care of your treasures not so much as a gold pin should ever be lost. Put this vain fellow to the test and throw the ring from the princess's finger into the brook, and bid him find it. We shall soon see what his talk is worth."

And the foolish king listened to them, and ordered the prince to be brought before him.

"My son," he said, "I have heard that you have declared that if I made you keeper of my treasures you would never lose so much as a gold pin. Now, in order to prove the truth of your words, I am going to throw the ring from the princess's finger into the brook. If you do not find it before I come back from council, you will have to die a horrible death."

It was no use denying that he had said anything of the

kind. The king did not believe him. In fact, he paid no attention at all and hurried off, leaving the poor boy speechless with despair in the corner. However, he soon remembered that though it was very unlikely that he should find the ring in the brook, it was impossible that he should find it by staying in the palace.

For some time the prince wandered up and down peering into the bottom of the stream, but though the water was very clear, nothing could he see of the ring. At length he gave it up in despair and, throwing himself down at the foot of the tree, he wept bitterly.

"What is the matter, dear prince?" said a voice just above him, and raising his head, he saw the wild duck.

"The king of this country declares I must die a horrible death if I cannot find the princess's ring which he has thrown into the brook," answered the prince.

"Oh, you must not worry about that, for I can help you," replied the bird. "I am the king of the wild ducks, whose life you spared, and now it is my turn to save yours." Then he flew away, and in a few minutes a great flock of ducks were swimming all up and down the stream looking for the ring with all their might. Long before the king came back from his council, there it was, safe on the grass beside the prince.

At this sight the king was yet more astonished at the cleverness of his steward, and at once promoted him to be the keeper of his jewels.

Now you would have thought that by this time the king would have been satisfied with the prince, and would have left him alone. But people's natures are very hard to change, and when the two envious soldiers came to him with a new falsehood, he was as ready to listen to them as before.

"Gracious Majesty," said they, "the youth whom you have made keeper of your jewels has declared to us that a child shall be born in the palace this night, which will be able to speak every language in the world and to play every instrument of music. Is he then become a prophet, or a magician, that he should know things which have not yet come to pass?"

At these words the king became more angry than ever. He had tried to learn magic himself, but somehow or other his spells would never work, and he was furious to hear that the prince claimed a power that he did not possess. Stammering with rage, he ordered the youth to be brought before him and vowed that unless this miracle was accomplished he would have the prince dragged from a horse's tail until he was dead.

In spite of what the soldiers had said, the boy knew no more magic than the king did, and his task seemed more hopeless than before. He lay weeping in the chamber which he was forbidden to leave, when suddenly he heard a sharp tapping at the window, and, looking up, he beheld a stork.

"What makes you so sad, prince?" asked he.

"Someone has told the king that I have prophesied that a child shall be born this night in the palace, who can speak all the languages in the world and play every musical instrument. I am no magician to bring these things to pass, but he says that if it does not happen he will have me dragged through the city from a horse's tail until I die."

"Do not trouble yourself," answered the stork. "I will manage to find such a child, for I am the king of the storks whose life you spared, and now I can repay you for it."

The stork flew away and soon returned carrying in his beak a baby wrapped in swaddling clothes and laid it down near a lute. In an instant the baby stretched out its little hands and began to play a tune so beautiful that even the prince forgot his sorrows as he listened. Then he was given a flute and a zither, and he was just as able to draw music from them. The prince, whose courage was gradually rising, spoke to him in all the languages he knew. The baby answered him in all, and no one could have told which was his native tongue!

The next morning the king went straight to the prince's room, and saw with his own eyes the wonders that the baby could do. "If your magic can produce such a baby," he said, "you must be greater than any wizard that ever lived, and shall have my daughter in marriage." The king commanded the ceremony to be performed without delay, and a splendid feast to be made for the bride and bridegroom. When it was over, he said to the prince, "Now that you are really my son, tell me, by what arts were you able to fulfill the tasks I set you?"

"My noble father-in-law," answered the prince, "I am ignorant of all spells and arts. But somehow I have always managed to escape the death which has threatened me." And he told the king how he had been forced to run away from his stepfather, and how he had spared the three birds, and had joined the two soldiers, who had from envy done their best to ruin him.

The king rejoiced in his heart that his daughter had married a prince and not a common man, and he chased the two soldiers away with whips, and told them that if they ever dared to show their faces across the borders of his kingdom, they should die the same death he had prepared for the prince.

EIGHT

The Princess of the Golden Castle

by Katherine Pyle

from *The Counterpane Fairy* (1898)

Teddy was all alone, for his mother had been up with him so much the night before that at about four o'clock in the afternoon she said that she was going to lie down for a little while.

The room where Teddy lay was very pleasant, with two big windows, and the furniture covered with gay old-fashioned India calico. His mother had set a glass of milk on the table beside his bed, and left the stair door ajar so that he could call Hannah, the cook, if he wanted anything, and then she had gone over to her own room.

The little boy had always enjoyed being ill, for then he was read aloud to and had lemonade, but this had been a real illness, and though he was better now, the doctor still would not let him have anything but milk and thin porridge. He was feeling rather lonely, too, though the fire crackled cheerfully, and he could hear Hannah singing to herself in the kitchen below.

Teddy turned over the pages of *Robinson Crusoe* for a while, looking at the colored pictures. Then he closed the book and called, "Hannah!" The singing in the kitchen below ceased, and Teddy knew that Hannah was listening. "Hannah!" he called again.

At the second call Hannah came hurrying up the stairs and into the room. "What do you want, Teddy?"

"Hannah, I want to ask Mamma something," said Teddy.

"Oh," said Hannah, "you wouldn't want me to call your poor mother, would you, when she was up with you the whole of last night and has just gone to lie down a bit?"

"I want to ask her something," repeated Teddy.

"You ask me what you want to know," suggested Hannah. "Your poor mother's so tired that I'm sure you are too much of a man to want me to call her."

"Well, I want to ask her if I may have a cracker," said Teddy.

"Oh, no; you couldn't have that," said Hannah. "Don't you know that the doctor said you mustn't have anything but milk and gruel? Did you want to ask her anything else?"

"No," said Teddy, and his lip trembled.

After that Hannah went downstairs to her work again, and Teddy lay staring out of the window at the windy gray clouds that were sweeping across the April sky. He grew lonelier and lonelier, and a lump rose in his throat. Soon a big tear trickled down his cheek and dripped off his chin.

"Oh dear, oh dear!" said a little voice just back of the hill his knees made as he lay with them drawn up in bed; "what a hill to climb!"

Teddy stopped crying and gazed in wonder toward where the voice came from. Presently, over the top of his knees appeared a brown peaked hood, a tiny withered face, a flapping brown cloak, and last of all two small feet in buckled shoes. It was a little old woman, so shrunken and brown that she looked more like a dried leaf than anything else.

She seated herself on Teddy's knees and gazed down at him solemnly. She was so light that he felt her weight no more than if she had been a feather.

Teddy lay staring at her for a while, and then he asked, "Who are you?"

"I'm the Counterpane* Fairy," said the little figure, in a thin voice.

"I don't know what that is," said Teddy.

"Well," said the Counterpane Fairy, "it's the sort of a fairy that lives in houses and watches out for the children. I used to be one of the court fairies, but I grew tired of that. There was nothing in it, you know."

---

* Counterpane: bedspread or quilt.

"Nothing in what?" asked Teddy.

"Nothing in the court life. All day the fairies were swinging in spider-webs and sipping honeydew, or playing games of hide-and-go-seek. The only comfort I had was with an old field-mouse who lived at the edge of the wood, and I used to spend a great deal of time with her. I used to take care of her babies when she was out hunting for something to eat. Cunning little things they were—five of them, all fat and soft, and with such funny little tails."

"What became of them?"

"Oh, they moved away. They left before I did. As soon as they were old enough, Mother field-mouse went. She said she couldn't stand the court fairies. They were always playing tricks on her, stopping up the door of her house with sticks and acorns, and making faces at her babies until they almost drove them into fits. So after that I left too."

"Where did you go?"

"Oh, hither and yon. Mostly where there were little sick boys and girls."

"Do you like little boys?"

"Yes, when they don't cry," said the Counterpane Fairy, staring at him very hard.

"Well, I was lonely," said Teddy. "I wanted my mamma."

"Yes, I know, but you oughtn't to have cried. I came to you, though, because you were lonely and sick, and I thought maybe you would like me to show you a story."

"Do you mean tell me a story?" asked Teddy.

"No," said the fairy, "I mean show you a story. It's a game I invented after I joined the Counterpane Fairies. Choose any one of the squares of the counterpane and I will show you how to play it. That's all you have to do—to choose a square."

Teddy looked the counterpane over carefully. "I think I'll choose that yellow square," he said, "because it looks so nice and bright."

"Very well," said the Counterpane Fairy. "Look straight at it and don't turn your eyes away until I count seven times seven and then you shall see the story of it."

Teddy fixed his eyes on the square and the fairy began to count. "One—two—three—four," she counted; Teddy heard her voice, thin and clear as the hissing of the logs on the hearth. "Don't look away from the square," she cried. "Five—six—seven"—it seemed to Teddy that the yellow silk square was turning to a mist before his eyes and wrapping everything about him in a golden glow. "Thirteen—fourteen"—the fairy counted on and on. "Forty-six—forty-seven—forty-eight—FORTY-NINE!"

At the words *forty-nine*, the Counterpane Fairy clapped her hands and Teddy looked about him. He was no longer in a golden mist. He was standing in a wonderful enchanted garden. The sky was like the golden sky at sunset, and the grass was so thickly set with tiny yellow flowers that it looked like a golden carpet. From this garden stretched a long flight of glass steps. They reached up and up and up to a great golden castle with shining domes and towers.

"Listen!" said the Counterpane Fairy. "In that golden castle there lies an enchanted princess. For more than a hundred years she has been lying there waiting for the hero who is to come and rescue her, and you are the hero who can do it if you will."

With that the fairy led him to a little pool close by, and told him to look in the water. When Teddy looked, he saw himself standing there in the golden garden, and he did not appear as he ever had before. He was tall and strong and beautiful, like a hero.

"Yes," said Teddy, "I will do it."

At these words, from the grass, the bushes, and the trees around, suddenly started a flock of golden birds. They circled about him and over him, clapping their wings and singing triumphantly. Their song reminded Teddy of the blackbirds that sang on the lawn at home in the early spring, when the daffodils were up. Then in a moment they were all gone, and the garden was still again.

Their song had filled his heart with a longing for great deeds. Without pausing longer, he ran to the glass steps and began to mount them.

Up and up and up he went. Once he turned and waved his hand to the Counterpane Fairy in the golden garden far below. She waved her hand in answer, and he heard her voice faint and clear. "Good-bye! Good-bye! Be brave and strong, and beware of that which is little and gray."

Then Teddy turned his face toward the castle, and in a moment he was standing before the great shining gates.

He raised his hand and struck bravely upon the door. There was no answer. Again he struck upon it, and his blow rang through the hall inside; then he opened the door and went in.

The hall was five-sided, and all of pure gold, as clear and shining as glass. Upon three sides of it were three arched doors; one was of emerald, one was of ruby, and one was of diamond; they were arched, and tall, and wide—fit for a hero to go through. The question was, behind which one lay the enchanted princess?

While Teddy stood there looking at them and wondering, he heard a little thin voice that seemed to be singing to itself, and this is what it sang:

In and out and out and in,
Quick as a flash I weave and spin.
Some may mistake and some forget,
But I'll have my spider-web finished yet.

When Teddy heard the song, he knew that someone must be awake in the enchanted castle, so he began looking about him.

On the fourth side of the wall there hung a curtain of silvery-gray spider-web, and the voice seemed to come from it.

The hero went toward it, but he saw nothing, for the spider that was spinning it moved so fast that no eyes could follow it. Presently it paused up in the left-hand corner of the web, and then Teddy saw it. It looked very little to have spun all that curtain of silvery web.

As Teddy stood looking at it, it began to sing again:

Here in my shining web I sit,
To look about and rest a bit.
I rest myself a bit and then,
Quick as a flash, I begin again.

"Mistress Spinner! Mistress Spinner!" cried Teddy. "Can you tell me where to find the enchanted princess who lies asleep waiting for me to come and rescue her?"

The spider sat quite still for a while, and then it said in a voice as thin as a hair: "You must go through the emerald door; you must go through the emerald door. What so fit as the emerald door for the hero who would do great deeds?"

Teddy did not so much as stay to thank the little gray spinner, he was in such a hurry to find the princess. Turning, he sprang to the emerald door, flung it open, and stepped outside.

He found himself standing on the glass steps, and as his foot touched the topmost one the whole flight closed up like an umbrella, and in a moment Teddy was sliding down the smooth glass pane, faster and faster and faster until he could hardly catch his breath.

The next thing he knew he was standing in the golden garden, and there was the Counterpane Fairy beside him looking at him sadly. "You should have known better than to try the emerald door," she said. "And now shall we end the story?"

"Oh, no, no!" cried Teddy, and he was still the hero. "Let me try once more, for it may be I can yet save the princess."

Then the Counterpane Fairy smiled. "Very well," she said, "you shall try again. But remember what I told you. Beware of that which is little and gray, and take this with you, for it may be of use." Stooping, she picked up a blade of grass from the ground and handed it to him.

The hero took it, and in his hands it was changed to a sword that shone so brightly that it dazzled his eyes. Then he turned, and there was the long flight of glass steps leading up to the golden castle just as before. Thrusting the magic sword into his belt, he ran nimbly up and up and up. Not until he reached the very topmost step did he turn and look back to wave farewell to the Counterpane Fairy below. She waved her hand to him. "Remember," she called, "beware of what is little and gray."

He opened the door and went into the five-sided golden hall, and there were the three doors just as before, and the spider spinning and singing on the fourth side:

Now the brave hero is wiser indeed;
He may have failed once, but he still may succeed.

Dull are the emeralds; diamonds are bright;
So is his wisdom that shines as the light.

"The diamond door!" cried Teddy. "Yes, that is the door that I should have tried. How could I have thought the emerald door was it?" and opening the diamond door he stepped through it.

He hardly had time to see that he was standing at the top of the glass steps, before—br-r-r-r!—they had shut up again into a smooth glass hill, and there he was spinning down them so fast that the wind whistled past his ears.

In less time than it takes to tell, he was back again for the third time in the golden garden, with the Counterpane Fairy standing before him, and he was ashamed to raise his eyes.

"So!" said the Counterpane Fairy. "Did you know no better than to open the diamond door?"

"No," said Teddy, "I knew no better."

"Then," said the fairy, "if you can pay no better attention to my warnings than that, the princess must wait for another hero, for you are not the one."

"Let me try but once more," cried Teddy, "for this time I shall surely find her."

"Then you may try once more and for the last time," said the fairy, "but beware of what is little and gray." Stooping, she picked from the grass beside her a fallen acorn cup and handed it to him. "Take this with you," she said, "for it may serve you well."

As he took it from her, it was changed in his hand to a goblet of gold set round with precious stones. He shoved it inside his shirt, for he was in a hurry, and turning he ran for the third time up the flight of glass steps. This time he was so eager that he never once paused to look back, but all the time he ran on up and up he was wondering what it was that she meant about her warning. She had said, "Beware of what is little and gray." What had he seen that was little and gray?

As soon as he reached the great golden hall he walked over to the curtain of spider-web. The spider was spinning so fast that it was little more than a gray streak, but presently it stopped up in the left-hand corner of the web. As the hero looked at it he saw that it was little and gray. Then it began to sing to him in its little thin voice:

Great hero, wiser than ever before,
Try the red door, try the red door.
Open the door that is ruby, and then
You never need search for the princess again.

"No, I will not open the ruby door," cried Teddy. "Twice have you sent me back to the golden garden, and now you shall fool me no more."

As he said this he saw that one corner of the spider-web curtain was still unfinished, in spite of the spider's haste, and underneath was something that looked like a little yellow door. Then suddenly he knew that was the door he must go through. He caught hold of the curtain and pulled, but it was as strong as steel. Quick as a flash he snatched from his belt the magic sword, and with one blow the curtain was cut in two, and fell at his feet.

He heard the little gray spider calling to him in its thin voice, but he paid no heed, for he had opened the little yellow door and bowed his head and entered.

Beyond was a great courtyard all of gold, and with a fountain leaping and splashing back into a golden basin in the middle. What he saw first of all was the enchanted princess, who lay stretched out as if asleep upon a couch all covered with cloth of gold. He knew she was a princess, because she was so beautiful and because she wore a golden crown.

He stood looking at her without stirring, and at last he whispered, "Princess! Princess! I have come to save you."

Still she did not stir. He bent and touched her, but she lay there in her enchanted sleep, and her eyes did not open. Then Teddy looked about him, and seeing the fountain he drew the magic cup from his shirt and, filling it, sprinkled the hands and face of the princess with the water.

Then her eyes opened and she raised herself upon her elbow and smiled. "Have you come at last?" she cried.

"Yes," answered Teddy, "I have come."

The princess looked about her. "But what became of the spider?" she said.

Then Teddy, too, looked about, and there was the spider running across the floor toward where the princess lay.

Quickly he sprang from her side and set his foot upon it. There was a thin squeak and then—there was nothing left of the little gray spinner but a tiny gray smudge on the floor.

Instantly the golden castle was shaken from top to bottom, and there was a sound of many voices shouting outside. The princess rose to her feet and caught the hero by the hand. "You have broken the enchantment," she cried, "and now you shall be the King of the Golden Castle and reign with me."

"Oh, but I can't," said Teddy, "because—because—"

But the princess drew him out with her through the hall, and there they were at the head of the flight of glass steps. A great host of soldiers and courtiers were running up it. They were dressed in cloth of gold, and they shouted at the sight of Teddy: "Hail to the hero! Hail to the hero!" Teddy recognized them by their voices as the golden birds that had fluttered around him in the garden below.

"And all this is yours," said the beautiful princess, turning toward him with—

* * *

"So that is the story of the yellow square," said the Counterpane Fairy.

Teddy looked about him. The golden castle was gone,

and the stairs, and the shouting courtiers. He was lying in bed with the silk coverlet over his little knees and Hannah was still singing in the kitchen below.

"Did you like it?" asked the fairy.

Teddy heaved a deep sigh. "Oh! Wasn't it beautiful?" he said. Then he lay for a while thinking and smiling. "Wasn't the princess lovely?" he whispered half to himself.

The Counterpane Fairy got up slowly and stiffly, and picked up the staff that she had laid down beside her. "Well, I must be journeying on," she said.

"Oh, no, no!" cried Teddy. "Please don't go yet."

"Yes, I must," said the Counterpane Fairy. "I hear your mother coming."

"But will you come back again?" cried Teddy.

The Counterpane Fairy made no answer. She was walking down the other side of the bedquilt hill, and Teddy heard her voice, little and thin, dying away in the distance: "Oh dear, dear, dear! What a hill to go down! What a hill it is! Oh dear, dear, dear!"

Then the door opened and his mother came in. She was looking rested, and she smiled at him lovingly, but the little brown Counterpane Fairy was gone.

NINE

The Gate of the Giant Scissors

by Annie Fellows Johnston

from *The Gate of the Giant Scissors* (1898)

Once upon a time, on a far island of the sea, there lived a King with seven sons. The three eldest were tall and dark, with eyes like eagles, and hair like a crow's wing for blackness, and no princes in all the land were so strong and fearless as they. The three youngest sons were tall and fair, with eyes as blue as cornflowers, and locks like the summer sun for brightness, and no princes in all the land were so brave and beautiful as they.

But the middle son was neither dark nor fair; he was neither handsome nor strong. When the King saw that he never won in the tournaments, nor led in the boar hunts, nor sang to his lute among the ladies of the court, he drew his royal robes around him, and frowned on Ethelried.

To each of his other sons he gave part of his kingdom, armor and plumes, a prancing charger, and a trusty sword; but to Ethelried he gave nothing. When the poor Prince saw his brothers riding out into the world to win their fortunes, he wanted to follow. Throwing himself on his knees before the King, he cried, "Oh royal Sire, bestow upon me also a sword and a steed, that I may follow my brothers."

But the King laughed him to scorn, "You, a sword!" he said. "You have never done a brave deed in all your life! In truth, you shall have one gift, but it shall be one that fits your maiden size and courage, if so small a weapon can be found in all my kingdom!"

Now just at that moment it happened that the Court Tailor came into the room to measure the King for a new mantle of ermine. Immediately the grinning jester began shrieking with laughter, so that the bells upon his cap were all set a-jangling.

"What now, Fool?" demanded the King.

"I did but laugh to think the sword of Ethelried had been so quickly found," said the jester, and he pointed to the scissors hanging from the Tailor's girdle.

"By my pledge," exclaimed the King, "it shall be even as you say!" He commanded that the scissors be taken from the Tailor, and buckled to the belt of Ethelried.

"Not until you have proved yourself a prince with these,

shall you come into your kingdom," he swore with a mighty oath. "Until that far day, now get you gone!"

So Ethelried left the palace and wandered away over mountain and moor with a heavy heart. No one knew that he was a prince; no fireside offered him welcome; no lips gave him a friendly greeting. The scissors hung useless and rusting by his side.

One night as he lay in a deep forest, too unhappy to sleep, he heard a noise near at hand in the bushes. By the light of the moon he saw that a ferocious wild beast had been caught in a hunter's trap and was struggling to free itself from the heavy net. His first thought was to kill the animal, for he had had no meat for many days. Then he thought that he had no weapon large enough.

While he stood gazing at the struggling beast, it turned to him with such a pleading look in its wild eyes that he was moved to pity.

"You shall have your liberty," he cried, "even though you may tear me in pieces the moment you are free. Better dead than this cowardly life to which my father has doomed me!"

Ethelried set to work with the little scissors to cut the great ropes of the net in two. At first, each strand seemed as hard as steel. The blades of the scissors were so rusty and dull that he could scarcely move them. Great beads of sweat stood out on his brow as he bent himself to the task.

Then, as he worked, the blades began to grow sharper

and sharper, and brighter and brighter, and longer and longer. By the time the last rope was cut, the scissors were as sharp as a broadsword and half as long as his body.

At last he raised the net to let the beast go free. Then he sank on his knees in astonishment. It had suddenly disappeared, and in its place stood a beautiful Fairy with filmy wings, which shone like rainbows in the moonlight.

"Prince Ethelried," she said in a voice that was like a crystal bell's for sweetness, "do you not know that you are in the domain of a frightful Ogre? He changed me into the form of a wild beast and set the snare to capture me. Without your fearlessness and faithful perseverance in trying to set me free, I would have died at dawn."

At this moment there was a distant rumbling like thunder. "It's the Ogre!" cried the Fairy. "We must hurry." Seizing the scissors that lay on the ground where Ethelried had dropped them, she opened and shut them several times, exclaiming:

Scissors, grow a giant's height
And save us from the Ogre's might!

Immediately they grew to an enormous size and, with blades extended, shot through the tangled thicket ahead of them, cutting down everything that stood in their way—bushes, stumps, trees, vines; nothing could stand before the fierce onslaught of those mighty blades.

FAERIE GOLD

The Fairy darted down the path thus opened up, and Ethelried followed as fast as he could, for the horrible roaring was rapidly coming nearer. At last they reached a wide chasm that bounded the Ogre's domain. Once across that, they would be out of his power, but it seemed impossible to cross.

Again the Fairy touched the scissors, saying:

Giant scissors, bridge the path,
And save us from the Ogre's wrath.

Again the scissors grew longer and longer, until they lay across the chasm like a shining bridge. Ethelried hurried across after the Fairy, trembling and dizzy, for the Ogre was now almost upon them. As soon as they were safe on the other side, the Fairy blew upon the scissors, and, presto, they became shorter and shorter until they were only the length of an ordinary sword.

"Here," she said, putting them into his hands. "Because you were persevering and fearless in setting me free, these shall win for you your heart's desire. But remember that you cannot keep them sharp and shining, unless they are used at least once each day in some unselfish service."

Before he could thank her she had vanished, and he was left in the forest alone. He could see the Ogre standing powerless to hurt him on the other side of the chasm, gnashing his teeth, each one of which was as big as a millstone.

The sight was so terrible that Ethelried fled away as fast

as his feet could carry him. By the time he reached the edge of the forest he was very tired and ready to faint from hunger. His heart's greatest desire was for food, and he wondered if the scissors could get it for him as the Fairy had promised. He had spent his last coin and knew not where to go for another.

Just then he spied a tree, hanging full of great, yellow apples. By standing on tiptoe he could barely reach the lowest one with his scissors. He cut off an apple and was about to take a bite when an old Witch sprang out of a hollow tree across the road.

"So you are the thief who has been stealing my gold apples for the past two weeks!" she exclaimed. "Well, you shall never steal again, that I promise you. Ho, Frog-eye Fearsome, seize on him and drag him into your darkest dungeon!"

At that, a hideous-looking fellow, with eyes like a frog's, green hair, and horrid clammy webbed fingers, clutched Ethelried before he could turn to defend himself. He was thrown into the dungeon and left there all day.

At sunset, Frog-eye Fearsome opened the door to slide in a crust of bread and a cup of water. In a croaking voice, he said, "You shall be hanged in the morning, hanged by the neck until you are quite dead." Then he stopped to run his webbed fingers through his damp green hair and grin at the poor captive Prince, as if he enjoyed his suffering. But the next morning no one came to take him to the gallows, and he sat all day in total darkness. At sunset Frog-eye Fearsome opened the door again to thrust in another crust and some water and say, "In the morning you shall be drowned; drowned in the Witch's mill-pond with a great stone tied to your feet."

Again the croaking creature stood and gloated over his victim, then left him to the silence of another long day in the dungeon. The third day he opened the door and hopped in, rubbing his webbed hands together with fiendish pleasure, saying, "You are to have no food and drink tonight, for the Witch has thought of a far more horrible punishment for you. In the morning I shall surely come again, and then—beware!"

As he stopped to grin once more at the poor Prince, a Fly darted in. Blinded by the darkness of the dungeon, it flew straight into a spider's web, above the head of Ethelried.

"Poor creature!" thought Ethelried. "You shall not be left a prisoner in this dismal spot while I have the power to help you." He lifted the scissors and with one stroke destroyed the web and gave the Fly its freedom.

As soon as the dungeon had stopped echoing with the noise that Frog-eye Fearsome made in banging shut the heavy door, Ethelried heard a low buzzing near his ear. It was the Fly, which had lit on his shoulder.

"Let an insect in its gratitude teach you this," buzzed the Fly. "Tomorrow, if you remain here, you must certainly meet your doom, for the Witch never keeps a prisoner past the third night. But escape is possible. Your prison door is made of iron, but the shutter which bars the window is only of wood. Cut your way out at midnight, and I will have a friend waiting to guide you to a place of safety. A faint glimmer of light on the opposite wall shows me the keyhole. I shall make my escape through it and go to repay your unselfish service to me. But know that the scissors move only when commanded in rhyme. Farewell."

The Prince spent all the following time until midnight trying to think of a suitable verse to say to the scissors. The art of rhyming had been neglected in his early education, and it was not until the first cock-crowing began that he succeeded in making this one:

Giant scissors, serve me well,
And save me from the Witch's spell!

As he spoke the words, the scissors leaped out of his hand and began to cut through the wooden shutters as easily as through cheese. In a very short time the Prince had crawled through the opening. There he stood, outside the dungeon, but it was a dark night and he knew not which way to turn.

He could hear Frog-eye Fearsome snoring like a tempest up in the watch-tower, and the old Witch was talking in her sleep in seven languages. While he stood looking around him in bewilderment, a Firefly alighted on his arm. Flashing its little lantern in the Prince's face, it cried, "This way! My friend, the Fly, sent me to guide you to a place of safety. Follow me and trust entirely to my direction."

The Prince flung his mantle over his shoulder and followed on with all possible speed. They stopped first in the Witch's orchard, and the Firefly held its lantern up while the Prince filled his pockets with the fruit. The apples were gold with emerald leaves, and the cherries were rubies, and the grapes were great bunches of amethyst. When the Prince had filled his pockets, he had enough wealth to provide for all his wants for at least a year.

The Firefly led him on until they came to a town where was a fine inn. There he left him and flew off to report the Prince's safety to the Fly and receive the promised reward.

Here Ethelried stayed for many weeks, living like a king on the money that the fruit jewels brought him. All this time the scissors were becoming little and rusty because he never once used them, as the Fairy had taught him, in unselfish service for others. But one day he remembered her command and went to seek some opportunity to help somebody.

Soon he came to a tiny hut where a sick man lay moaning, while his wife and children wept beside him. "What is to become of me?" cried the poor peasant. "My grain must fall and rot in the field from over-ripeness because I do not have the strength to rise and harvest it. Then we will all starve."

Ethelried heard him, and that night when the moon rose he stole into the field to cut it down with the giant scissors. They were so rusty from long idleness that he could scarcely move them. He tried to think of some rhyme with which to command them, but it had been so long since he had done any thinking, except for his own selfish pleasure, that his brain refused to work.

However, he worked on all night, slowly cutting down the grain stalk by stalk. Towards morning the scissors became brighter and sharper, until they finally began to open and shut on their own. The whole field was cut by sunrise. Now the peasant's wife had risen very early to go down to the spring and dip up some cool water for her husband to drink. She came upon Ethelried as he was cutting the last row of the grain, and fell on her knees to thank him. From that day, the peasant and all his family were Ethelried's friends and would have gone through fire and water to serve him.

After that he had many adventures, and he was very busy, for he never again forgot what the Fairy had said, that only unselfish service each day could keep the scissors sharp and shining. When the shepherd lost a little lamb one day on the mountain, it was Ethelried who found it caught by its fleece in a tangle of cruel thorns. When he had cut it loose and carried it home, the shepherd also became his firm friend, and would have gone through fire and water to serve him.

The old woman whom he supplied with bundles of wood, the merchant whom he rescued from robbers, the King's counselor to whom he gave aid—all became his friends. Up and down the land, to beggar or lord, homeless wanderer or highborn lady, he gladly gave unselfish service without being asked, and such as he helped immediately became his friends.

Day by day the scissors grew sharper and sharper and ever more quick to spring forward at his command.

One day a herald dashed down the highway, shouting through his silver trumpet that a beautiful Princess had been carried away by the Ogre. She was the only child of the King of this country, and the knights and nobles of all other realms and all the royal potentates were asked to come to her rescue. The one who could bring her back to her father's castle should be given the throne and kingdom, as well as the Princess herself.

From far and near, indeed from almost every country under the sun, came knights and princes to fight the Ogre. One by one their brave heads were cut off and stuck on poles along the moat that surrounded the castle.

Still the beautiful Princess suffered in her prison. Every night at sunset she was taken up to the roof for a glimpse of the sky and told to say goodbye to the sun, for the next morning would surely be her last. Then she would wring her lily-white hands and wave a sad farewell to her home, lying far to the westward. When the knights saw this they would rush down to the chasm and sound a challenge to the Ogre.

They were brave men, and they would not have feared to meet the fiercest wild beasts, but many shrank back when the Ogre came rushing out. They dared not meet in single combat this monster with the gnashing teeth, each one of which was as big as a millstone.

Among those who drew back were Ethelried's brothers (the three that were dark and the three that were fair). They would not admit their fear. They said, "We are only waiting to lay some wily plan to capture the Ogre."

After several days, Ethelried reached the place on foot. "See him," laughed one of the brothers that was dark to one that was fair. "He comes on foot—no prancing horse, no waving plumes, no trusty sword; little and lorn, he is not fit to be called a brother to princes."

But Ethelried ignored their mocking. He dashed across the drawbridge, and, opening his scissors, cried:

Giant scissors, rise in power!
Grant me my heart's desire this hour!

The crowds on the other side held their breath as the Ogre rushed out, waving a club as big as a church steeple. Then, "Whack! Bang!" The blows of the scissors, fighting off the blows of the mighty club, could be heard for miles around.

At last Ethelried became so exhausted that he could scarcely raise his hand, and it was plain to see that the scissors could not do battle much longer. By this time a great many people, attracted by the terrific noise, had come running up to the moat. The news had spread far and wide that Ethelried was in danger; so all those he had ever served dropped whatever they were doing and ran to the scene of the battle. The peasant was there, and the shepherd, and the lords and beggars and highborn ladies, all those whom Ethelried had ever befriended.

When they saw that the poor Prince was about to be defeated, they all cried out bitterly. "He saved my harvest," cried one. "He found my lamb," cried another. "He showed me a greater kindness still," shouted a third. And so they went on, each telling of some unselfish service that the Prince had given. Their voices all joined into such a roar of gratitude that the scissors were given fresh strength on account of it. They grew longer and longer, and stronger and stronger, until with one great swoop they sprang forward and cut the ugly old Ogre's head from his shoulders.

Every cap was thrown up, and such cheering rent the air as has never been heard since. They did not know his name, they did not know that he was Prince Ethelried, but they knew by his valor that there was royal blood in his veins. So they all cried out long and loud: "Long live the Prince! Prince Ciseaux!"

Then the King stepped down from his throne and took off his crown to give to the conqueror, but Ethelried put it aside.

"No," he said. "The only kingdom that I long for is the kingdom of a loving heart and a happy fireside. Keep all but the Princess."

So the Ogre was killed, and the prince came into the kingdom that was his heart's desire. He married the Princess, and there was feasting and merrymaking for seventy days and seventy nights, and they all lived happily ever after.

When the feasting was over and the guests had all gone to their homes, the Prince pulled down the house of the Ogre and built a new one. On every gable he fastened a pair of shining scissors to remind himself that only through unselfish service to others comes the happiness that is highest and best.

Over the great entrance gate he hung the ones that had served him so valiantly, saying, "Only those who belong to the kingdom of loving hearts and happy homes can ever enter here."

One day the old King, with the brothers of Ethelried (the three that were dark and the three that were fair), came riding up to the portal. They expected to share in Ethelried's fame and splendor. But the scissors leaped from their place and snapped so angrily in their faces that they turned their horses and fled.

Then the scissors sprang back to their place again to guard the gateway of Ethelried. To this day, only those who belong to the kingdom of loving hearts may enter the Gate of the Giant Scissors.

PART FOUR

JUST REWARDS

Alas! How easily things go wrong!
A sign too much or a kiss too long,
And then follows a mist and weeping rain,
And life is never the same again.
　　—**George MacDonald,** *Phantastes*

TEN

The Greedy Shepherd

by Frances Browne

from *Granny's Wonderful Chair* (1857)

Once upon a time there lived in the south country two brothers, whose business it was to keep sheep on a great grassy plain, which was bounded on the one side by a forest, and on the other by a chain of high hills. No one lived on that plain but shepherds, who dwelt in low cottages thatched with heath. They watched their sheep so carefully that no lamb was ever lost. None of the shepherds ever traveled beyond the foot of the hills and the skirts of the forest.

There were none among them more careful than two brothers, one of whom was called Clutch and the other Kind. Though born brothers, two men of distant countries could not be more unlike in character. Clutch thought of nothing in this world but how to catch and keep some profit for himself, while Kind would have shared his last bite of food with a hungry dog. Clutch's greedy mind made him keep all his father's sheep when the old man was dead and gone, because he was the oldest brother. He let Kind have nothing but the place of a servant to help him in looking after the sheep. Kind wouldn't quarrel with his brother for the sake of the sheep, so he helped him to keep them, and Clutch had all his own way. This made him agreeable. For some time the brothers lived peaceably in their father's cottage, which stood low and lonely under the shadow of a great sycamore tree. They kept their flock with pipe and crook on the grassy plain, until new troubles arose through Clutch's greediness.

On that plain there was no town, nor city, nor marketplace, where people might sell or buy, but the shepherds cared little for trade. The wool of their flocks made them clothes; their milk gave them butter and cheese. At feast times every family killed a lamb or so; their fields yielded them wheat for bread. The forest supplied them with firewood for winter; and every midsummer, which is the sheep-shearing time, traders from a certain far-off city came by an ancient path to purchase all the wool the shepherds could spare, and give them in exchange either goods or money.

One midsummer it so happened that these traders praised the wool of Clutch's flock above all they found on the plain, and gave him the highest price for it. That was an unlucky happening for the sheep. From then on Clutch thought he could never get enough wool off them. At the shearing time nobody clipped so close. In spite of all Kind could do or say, Clutch left the poor sheep as bare as if they had been shaved. As soon as the wool grew long enough to keep them warm, he was ready with the shears again—no matter how chilly might be the days or how near the winter. Kind didn't like these doings, and many an argument they caused between him and his brother. Clutch always tried to persuade him that close clipping was good for the sheep, and Kind always tried to make him think he had got all the wool. They were never done with disputes. Still Clutch sold the wool and stored up his profits, and one midsummer after another passed. The shepherds began to think him a rich man, and close clipping might have become the fashion, except for a strange thing which happened to his flock.

The wool had grown well that summer. He had taken two crops off them and was thinking of a third even though the misty mornings of autumn had come, and the cold evenings made the shepherds put on their winter cloaks. About that time, first the lambs and then the ewes began to stray away. Search as the brothers would, none of them was ever found again. Clutch blamed Kind with being careless and watched with all his might. Kind knew it was not his fault, but he looked sharper than ever.

Still the straying went on. The flocks grew smaller every

day, and all the brothers could find out was that the closest clipped were the first to go. No matter how carefully they watched the flock, some were sure to be missed when they gathered them into the fold.

Kind grew tired of watching, and Clutch lost his sheep with anger. The other shepherds, over whom he had boasted of his wool and his profits, were not sorry to see pride having a fall. Most of them pitied Kind, but all of them agreed that the brothers had marvelous bad fortune, and they kept as far from them as they could for fear of sharing it. Still the flock melted away as the months wore on. Storms and cold weather never stopped them from straying, and when the spring came back nothing remained with Clutch and Kind but three old ewes, the quietest and lamest of their whole flock.

They were watching these ewes one evening in the primrose time when Clutch, who had never kept his eyes off them that day, said, "Brother, there is wool to be had on their backs."

"It is too little to keep them warm," said Kind. "The east wind still blows sometimes." But Clutch was off to the cottage for the bag and shears.

Kind was grieved to see his brother so covetous, and to divert his mind he looked up at the great hills. It was a sort of comfort to him, ever since their losses began, to look at them evening and morning. Now their far-off heights were growing crimson with the setting sun, but as he looked, three creatures like sheep rushed up a gap in one of them as fleet as any deer. When Kind turned, he saw his brother coming with the bag and shears, but not a single ewe was to be seen.

Clutch's first question was, what had become of them. When Kind told him what he saw, the eldest brother scolded him fiercely for ever lifting his eyes off them. "Much good the hills and the sunset do us," he said, "now that we have not a single sheep. The other shepherds will hardly give us room among them at shearing time or harvest. I'll not stay on this plain to be despised for poverty. If you want to come with me and be guided by my advice, we shall get jobs somewhere. I have heard my father say that there were great shepherds living in old times beyond the hills. Let us go and see if they will take us for sheep-boys."

Kind would rather have stayed and tilled his father's wheat field, close by the cottage. But since his elder brother would go, he decided to keep him company. Next morning Clutch took his bag and shears, Kind took his crook and pipe, and away they went over the plain and up the hills. All who saw them thought that they had lost their senses, for no shepherd had gone there for a hundred years, and nothing was to be seen but wide moorlands, full of rugged rocks, and sloping up, it seemed, to the very sky. Kind persuaded his brother to take the direction the sheep had taken, but the ground was so rough and steep that after two hours' climbing they would gladly have turned back, if it had not been that their sheep were gone, and the shepherds would laugh at them.

By noon they came to the stony cleft, up which the three old ewes had run like deer. Both were tired and sat down to rest. Their feet were sore, and their hearts were heavy. As they sat there, there came a sound of music down the hills, as if a thousand shepherds had been playing on their tops. Clutch and Kind had never heard such music before. As they listened, the soreness passed from their feet, and the heaviness from their hearts. They arose and followed the sound up the cleft and over a wide heath covered with purple bloom. At sunset, they came to the hilltop and saw a broad pasture, where violets grew thick among the grass and thousands of snow-white sheep were feeding. An old man sat in the midst of them, playing on his pipe. He wore a long coat, the color of the holly leaves. His hair hung to his waist, and his beard to his knees, and both were as white as snow. He had the face of one who has led a quiet life and known no cares nor losses.

"Good father," said Kind, for his elder brother hung back and was afraid, "tell us what land is this, and where can we find service? My brother and I are shepherds and can well keep flocks from straying, though we have lost our own."

"These are the hill pastures," said the old man, "and I am the ancient shepherd. My flocks never stray, but I have employment for you. Which of you can shear best?"

"Good father," said Clutch, taking courage, "I am the closest shearer in all the country. You would not find as much wool as would make a thread on a sheep when I have finished with it."

"You are the man for my business," replied the old shepherd. "When the moon rises, I will call the flock you have to shear. Until then sit down and rest, and take your supper out of my bag."

Clutch and Kind gladly sat down by him among the violets. Opening a leather bag which hung by his side, the old man gave them cakes and cheese, and a horn cup to drink from a nearby stream. The brothers felt ready for any work after that meal. Clutch rejoiced in his own mind at the chance he had got for showing his skill with the shears. *Kind will see how useful it is to cut close*, he thought to himself. But they sat with the old man, telling him the news of the plain, till the sun went down and the moon rose, and all the sheep gathered and laid themselves down behind him. The old man then took his pipe and played a merry tune. Immediately there was heard a great howling, and up the hills came a troop of shaggy wolves, with hair so long that their eyes could scarcely be seen. Clutch would have fled for fear, but the wolves stopped, and the old man said to him, "Rise and shear—this flock of mine have too much wool on them."

Clutch had never shorn wolves before, yet he couldn't think of losing the good job, and went forward with a stout heart. The first wolf showed his teeth, and all the rest raised such a howl the moment Clutch came near them that he was glad to throw down his shears and run behind the old man for safety.

"Good father," he cried, "I will shear sheep, but not wolves."

"They must be shorn," said the old man, "or you go back to the plains, and them after you. Whichever of you can shear them will get the whole flock."

On hearing this, Clutch began to exclaim on his hard fortune, and his brother who had brought him there to be hunted and devoured by wolves. Kind, thinking that things could be no worse, caught up the shears he had thrown away in his fright, and went boldly up to the nearest wolf. To his great surprise the wild creature seemed to know him and stood quietly to be shorn, while the rest of the flock gathered round as if waiting their turn. Kind clipped neatly, but not too close, as he had wished his brother to do with the sheep, and heaped up the hair on one side. When he had done with one, another came forward, and Kind went on shearing by the bright moonlight until the whole flock was shorn.

Then the old man said, "You have done well. Take the wool and the flock for your wages. Return with them to the plain, and if you please, take this little-worth brother of yours for a boy to keep them."

Kind did not much like keeping wolves, but before he could answer, they had all changed into the very sheep which had strayed away so strangely. All of them had grown fatter and thicker of fleece, and the hair he had cut off lay by his side, a heap of wool so fine and soft that its like had never been seen on the plain.

Clutch gathered it up in his empty bag, glad to go back to the plain with his brother. The old man sent them away with their flock, saying no man must see the dawn of day on that pasture but himself, for it was the ground of the fairies. So Clutch and Kind went home with great gladness. All the shepherds came to hear their wonderful story, and ever after liked to keep near them because they had such good luck. They keep the sheep together until this day, but Clutch has grown less greedy, and Kind alone uses the shears.

ELEVEN

Flora's Birthday Party

by Christina Rossetti

from *Speaking Likenesses* (1874)

W hoever saw Flora on her birthday, at half-past seven
o'clock that morning, saw a very pretty sight. Eight
years old to a minute, and not awake yet. Her cheeks were
plump and pink, her light hair was all tumbled, her lips were
held together as if to kiss someone. Her eyes also, if you could
have seen them, were blue and merry, but for the moment
they had gone fast asleep and out of sight under fat little eye-
lids. Wagga the dog was up and about. Muff the cat was up
and about. Chirping birds were up and about on that summer morning. Only Flora slept on, and dreamed on, and never
stirred.

Her mother stooped over the child's soft bed and woke her

with a kiss. "Good morning, my darling, I wish you many and many happy returns of the day," said the kind, dear mother. Flora woke up to a sense of sunshine, and of pleasure full of hope.

On the breakfast table lay presents for Flora: a story-book full of pictures from her father, a writing-case from her mother, a golden pincushion like a hedgehog from her nurse, a box of sugarplums and a doll from Alfred her brother and Susan her sister—the most tempting of sugar plums, the most beautiful of curly-haired dolls, they appeared in her eyes.

A further treat was in store. "Flora," said her mother, "I have asked Richard, George, Anne, and Emily to spend the day with you and with Susan and Alfred. You are to be queen of the feast, because it is your birthday; and I trust you will all be very good and happy together."

Flora loved her brother and sister, her friend Emily, and her cousins Richard, George, and Anne. They had often played together before, and now if ever, surely on this special occasion they would play pleasantly together.

Anne with her brothers arrived first. Emily made her appearance soon after accompanied by a young friend, who was spending the holidays with her, and whom she introduced as Serena.

Emily brought Flora a sweet-smelling bouquet of flowers. Serena declared that Flora was the most charming girl she had ever met, except of course dearest Emily.

"Love me," said Serena, throwing her arms round her small hostess. "I will love you so much if you will only let me love you." Serena went on to exclaim over Flora's most elegant house. She said the lawn was a perfect park, and that Flora's older brother and sister amazed her with their cleverness. For the moment, silly little Flora felt quite tall and superior, and allowed herself to be loved very graciously.

After the arrivals and the settling down, there remained half an hour before dinner, for visiting and showing off presents. Flora displayed her doll and handed round her sugarplum box. "You took more than I did and it isn't fair," grumbled George at Richard.

Richard retorted, "Why, I saw you picking out the big ones."

"Oh," whined Anne, "I'm sure there were no big ones left when they came to me."

Emily put in with a smile of superiority, "Nonsense, Anne! You got the box before Serena and I did, and we don't complain."

"But there wasn't one," persisted Anne.

"But there were dozens and dozens," mimicked George, "only you're such a greedy little baby."

"Not one," whimpered Anne.

Then Serena remarked soothingly, "The sugarplums were most delicious, and now let us admire the lovely doll. Why, Flora, she must have cost pounds and pounds."

Flora, who had begun to look regretful, brightened up and said, "I don't know what she cost, but her name is Flora, and she has red boots with soles. Look at me opening and shutting her eyes, and I can make her say Mamma. Isn't she a beauty?"

"I never saw half such a beauty," replied smooth Serena. Then the party sat down to dinner.

Was it fact? Was it fancy? Each dish in turn was only fit to be found fault with. Meat underdone, potatoes overdone, beans splashy, jam tart not sweet enough, fruit all stone; covers clattering, glasses reeling, a fork or two dropping on the floor. Were these things really so? Or would even finest strawberries and richest cream have been found fault with, thanks to the children's mood that day?

Sad to say, what followed was a wrangle. An hour after dinner, blindman's bluff in the garden began well. But then Flora fell down and accused Alfred of tripping her up. Richard bawled out that George broke away when fairly caught. Anne, when held tight, muttered that Susan could see in spite of the blindfold over her eyes. Susan let go, and Alfred picked up his little sister. George volunteered to play blindman in Susan's stead. But still, pouting and grumbling showed their ugly faces, and tossed the apple of discord to and fro as if it had been a pretty plaything.

Would you like a game of hide-and-seek in a garden, where there are plenty of excellent hiding places and all sorts of pretty flowers to glance at while one goes seeking? These children on this particular day could not find it in their hearts to like it. Serena pretended to be afraid of searching along the dusky yew alley unless Alfred went with her, and at the very same moment Flora was determined to have him lift her up to look down into a hollow tree in which it was quite obvious Susan could not possibly have hidden. "It's my birthday," cried Flora. "It's my birthday."

George and Richard pushed each other roughly about till one slipped on the gravel walk and scratched his hands. They both turned cross and quit playing. At last, in sheer despair Susan stepped out of her hiding place behind the summer house. But even then she did her best to please everybody, for she brought in her hand a basket full of ripe mulberries which she had picked up off the grass as she stood in hiding.

Then they all set to running races across the smooth sloping lawn—until Anne tumbled down and cried, though she was not a bit hurt; and Flora, who was winning the race against Anne, thought herself mistreated and so sat and sulked. Then Emily smiled, but not good-naturedly. George and Richard each stuck a finger into one of each other's eyes and made faces at the two cross girls. Serena fanned herself, and Alfred looked at Susan, and Susan at Alfred, fairly at their wits' end.

An hour yet before tea-time: would another hour ever be over? Two little girls looking sullen, two little boys looking provoking: the sight was not at all an encouraging one. At last Susan took pouting Flora and tearful Anne by the hand and set off with them for a walk about the grounds. Meanwhile, Alfred fairly dragged Richard and George after the girls, and Emily arm-in-arm with Serena strolled beside them.

The afternoon was sunny, shady, breezy, warm, all at once. Bees were humming and harvesting as any bee of sense must have done among so many blossoms. Leafy boughs danced with the children's dancing shadows. Bellflowers rang without clappers. Now and then a pigeon cooed its soft water-bottle note, and a long way off sheep stood bleating.

Susan let go the little hot hands she held. As she walked she began telling a story to which all her companions soon paid attention—all except Flora.

Poor little Flora. Was this the end of her birthday? Was she eight years old at last only for this? Her sugarplums almost all gone and not cared for, her chosen pie not a nice one, herself so cross and miserable. Is it really worthwhile to be eight years old and have a birthday if this is what comes of it?

"—So the frog did not know how to boil the kettle, but he only replied, 'I can't bear hot water,' " went on Susan, telling her story. But Flora had no heart to listen, or to care about the frog. She lagged and dropped behind, not noticed by any one, creeping along slowly and sadly by herself.

Down the yew alley she turned, and it looked dark and

very gloomy as she passed out of the sunshine into the shadow. There were twenty yew trees on each side of the path, as she had counted over and over again a great many years ago when she was learning to count. But now at her right hand there stood twenty-one. And if the last tree was really a yew tree at all, it was at least a very odd one, for a lamp grew on its topmost branch. Never before either had the yew walk led to a door, but now at its further end stood a door with bell and knocker, and "Ring also" printed in black letters on a brass plate, all as plain as possible in the lamplight.

Flora stretched up her hand, and knocked and rang also.

She was surprised to feel the knocker shake hands with her, and to see the bell handle twist round and open the door. *Dear me*, she thought, *why couldn't the door open itself instead of bothering the bell?* But she only said, "Thank you," and walked in.

The door opened into a large and lofty apartment, very handsomely furnished. All the chairs were stuffed armchairs, and they moved their arms and shifted their shoulders to suit their sitters. All the sofas arranged and rearranged their pillows as convenience required. Footstools glided about, and rose or sank to meet every length of leg. Tables were no less helpful, and ran on noiseless rollers here or there when wanted. Tea trays set with saucers of strawberries, jugs of cream, and plates of cake floated in, settled down, and floated out again empty. They came and went politely through a square hole high up in one wall, beyond which lay the kitchen. Two harmoniums, an accordion, a pair of kettledrums and a peal of bells played together behind a screen, but kept silence during conversation. Photographs and pictures made the tour of the apartment, standing still when glanced at and going on when done with. In case of need the furniture flattened itself against the wall, and cleared the floor for a game, or for a dance. Flora noticed some of these remarkable details in the first few minutes after her arrival; some came to light as time went on. The only uncomfortable point in the room, that is, as to furniture, was that both ceiling and walls were lined throughout with looking-glasses. But at first this did not strike Flora as any disadvantage; indeed she thought it quite delightful, and took a long look at her little self full-length.

The room was full of boys and girls, older and younger, big and little. They all sat drinking tea at a great number of different tables; here half a dozen children sitting together, here more or fewer. Here one child would sit all alone at a table just the size for one comfortably. The tables were like telescope tables; only they expanded and contracted of themselves without extra pieces, and seemed to study everybody's convenience.

Every single boy and girl stared hard at Flora and went on staring. But not one of them offered her a chair, or a cup of tea, or anything else whatever. She grew very red and uncomfortable under so many staring pairs of eyes. Then a chair did what it could to relieve her embarrassment by pressing gently against her until she sat down. It bulged out its back comfortably into hers, and drew in its arms to suit her small size. A footstool grew somewhat taller beneath her feet. A table ran up with tea for one; a cream jug toppled over upon a saucerful of strawberries, and then righted itself again; the due quantity of sifted sugar sprinkled itself over the whole.

Flora could not help thinking everyone very rude and unpleasant to go on staring without speaking. She felt shy at having to eat with so many eyes upon her. Still, she was hot and thirsty, and the feast looked most tempting. She took up in a spoon one very large strawberry with plenty of cream; and was just putting it into her mouth when a voice called out crossly, "She shan't, they're mine." The spoon dropped from her startled hand, but without any clatter. Flora looked around to see the speaker.

The speaker was a girl seated in an extra-high armchair, with a stool as high as an ottoman under her feet, and a table as high as a chest of drawers in front of her. Perched upon her hair she wore a crown made of tinsel. Her face was a red face with a scowl. Sometimes perhaps she had looked nice and pretty, but this time she looked ugly. "You shan't, they're mine," she repeated in a cross, grumbling voice. "It's my birthday, and everything is mine."

Flora was too honest a little girl to eat strawberries that

were not given her or take even a cup of tea without permission. The table glided away with its delicious untasted load, and the armchair gave her a very gentle hug as if to comfort her.

If she could only have discovered the door, Flora would have fled through it back into the gloomy yew tree walk, and there have moped in solitude, rather than remain where she was not made welcome. But either the door was gone, or else it was shut to and lost amongst the multitude of mirrors. The birthday Queen, reflected over and over again in five hundred mirrors, looked frightful. Flora's fifty million reflections appeared flushed and angry too, but she soon tried to smile and succeeded, though she could not manage to feel very merry.

The meal ended at last. Most of the children had eaten and stuffed quite greedily. Poor Flora alone had not tasted a morsel. Then with a word and a kick from the Queen, her high footstool scudded away into a corner, and all the furniture arranged itself as flat as possible round the room, close up against the walls.

All the children now clustered together in the middle of the empty floor, elbowing and jostling each other, and arguing about what game should first be played. Flora, elbowed and jostled in their midst, noticed details of appearance that quite surprised her. Was it the children themselves, or was it their clothes? One boy bristled with prickly quills like a porcupine, and raised or lowered them at pleasure, but he usually kept them pointed outwards. Another, instead of being rounded like most people, had very sharp angles. A third caught in everything he came near, for he was hung round with hooks like fishhooks. One girl oozed a sticky fluid and came off on the fingers. Another, rather smaller, was slimy and slipped through the hands. Such exceptional features proved awkward, yet patience and tolerance might still have done something towards keeping matters smooth. But these unhappy children seemed not to know what forbearance or patience were.

"Tell us some new game," growled Hooks threateningly, catching in Flora's hair and tugging to get loose.

Flora did not at all like being spoken to in such a tone, and the hook hurt her very much. Still, though she could not think of anything new, she tried to do her best, and in a timid voice suggested "Les Graces."

"That's a girl's game," said Hooks contemptuously.

"It's as good any day as a boy's game," retorted Sticky.

"I wouldn't give *that* for your girl's games," snarled Hooks, trying to snap his fingers, but entangling two hooks and stamping.

"Poor dear fellow!" drawled Slime, pretending sympathy.

"It's quite as good," harped on Sticky. "It's as good or better."

Angles caught and would have shaken Slime, but she slipped through his fingers.

"Think of something else, and let it be new," yawned Quills.

"I really don't know anything new," answered Flora, half crying. She was going to add, "But I will play with you at any game you like, if you will teach me," when they all burst forth into a yell of "Cry, baby, cry! Cry, baby, cry!" They shouted it, screamed it, sang it. They pointed fingers, made faces, nodded heads at her. The wonder was she did not cry outright.

Finally the Queen said, "Let her alone. Who's she? It's *my* birthday, and we'll play at Hunt the Pincushion."

So Hunt the Pincushion it was. This game is simple and demands only a fair amount of skill. Select the smallest and weakest player (if possible let her be fat), chase her round and round the room, overtaking her at short intervals, and sticking pins into her here or there as it happens. Repeat, until you choose to catch and swing her, which concludes the game. Shortcuts, yells, and sudden leaps give spirit to the hunt.

The Pincushion was poor little Flora. How she strained and ducked and swerved to this side or that in an effort to escape her tormentors! Quills with every quill erect tilted against her and didn't need a pin. Angles whose corners almost cut, Hooks who caught and slit her frock, Slime who slid against and passed her, Sticky who rubbed off on her neck and plump bare arms, the scowling Queen, and the whole laughing, scolding, pushing troop, all carried long sharp pins, and all by turns overtook her. Finally the Queen caught her, swung her violently around, and let go suddenly. Flora, losing her balance, dropped upon the floor. But at least that game was over. And the carpet grew to such a depth of velvet pile below her that she fell quite lightly.

In that dreadful sport of Hunt the Pincushion, Flora was still better off than her stickers. In the thick of the throng they exasperated each other and fairly maddened themselves by a free use of cutting corners, pricking quills, catching hooks, glue, slime, and who knows what else. Slime, perhaps, would seem not so bad for its owner, but if a slimy person cannot be held, neither can she hold fast. As to Hooks and Sticky, often in wrenching themselves loose they got worse damage than they caused. The Queen was let off from particular personal pains, but then, it was her birthday! And she must still have suffered a good deal from the odd behavior of her subjects.

The next game called for was Self-Help. In this game, each boy depended completely on his own resources. Thus pins were forbidden, but every natural advantage—as a quill or fishhook—might be used to the maximum.

The boys were players, the girls were played (if I may be allowed such a phrase), all except the Queen who looked on and merely gave a slap or a box on the ear now and then to someone coming handy. Hooks shone in this sport and dragged about with him a load of attached captives, all struggling to unhook themselves. Angles crimped or creased several children by continued pressure. Quills could do little more than prick and scratch with some permanent results. Angles tore, pressed, and plaited Flora's dress in quite an unusual fashion. But this was better than her experience as Pincushion, and she bore it like a philosopher.

The boys did not as a whole get unmixed pleasure from their game of Self-Help, since there was much squabbling and some blows. The Queen did, perhaps, taste of fun without pain; but if so, she stood alone in satisfaction as in dignity.

The Queen yawned a very wide, loud yawn, and as everyone yawned in sympathy the game died out.

A supper table now moved from the wall to the middle of the floor, and armchairs enough gathered around it to seat the whole party. Through the square hole—not, alas! through the door of poor Flora's recollection—floated in the necessary number of plates, glasses, knives, forks, and spoons, along with many dishes and bottles filled with nice things.

This time Flora would not take so much as a fork without permission. Since the Queen paid not the slightest attention to her, she could only look hungrily on while the rest of the company feasted, and while dainties one after another placed themselves before her and left untasted—cold turkey, lobster salad, stewed mushrooms, raspberry tart, cream cheese, a meringue, a strawberry ice, sugared pineapple, some greengages. It may have been quite as well for her that she did not feel free to eat such a mixture, but it was tantalizing to watch so many good things come and go without taking even one taste, and to see all her companions stuffing without limit. Several of the boys seemed to think nothing of a whole turkey at a time, and the Queen ate one quart of strawberry ice, three pineapples, two melons, a score of meringues, and about four dozen sticks of angelica, as Flora counted.

After supper there was no need for the furniture to withdraw because the whole birthday party dropped out through a door (but still not through Flora's door) into a large playground. What they usually played I cannot tell you, but on this occasion a great number of bricks happened to be lying about on all sides mixed up with many neat piles of stones, so the children began building houses. Only instead of building from the outside as most bricklayers do, they built from the inside, taking care to have at hand plenty of bricks as well as good heaps of stones, and enclosing both themselves and the heaps as they built; one child with one heap of stones inside each house.

Strictly speaking, there were no bricks at all in the playground, only brick-shaped pieces of glass. Each of these had the sides brilliantly polished; while the edges, which were meant to touch and join, had a certain tenacity. There were bricks (so to call them) of all colors and many different shapes and sizes. Some were fancy bricks shaped in open work, some were engraved in running patterns, and others were cut into facets or blown into bubbles. A single house might have its blocks all uniform, or of twenty different fashions.

Yet, despite this amount of variety, every house built looked much like its neighbor: colors varied, architecture agreed. Four walls, no roof, no upper floor—such was each house, and it needed neither window nor staircase.

All this building took a long time, and gradually a very brilliant effect indeed was produced. The glass blocks were of beautiful tints, so that some houses glowed like masses of ruby, and others shone like enormous chrysolites or sapphires. Others showed the milkiness and fiery spark of a hundred opals, or glimmered like moonstone. The playground was lighted up, high, low, and on all sides, with colored lamps. Picture to yourselves golden twinkling lamps like stars high overhead, bluish twinkling lamps like glowworms down almost on the ground; lamps like illuminated peaches, apples, apricots, plums, hung about with the abundance of a most fruitful orchard.

To Flora's complete dismay, she found that she was being built in with the Queen. She was not asked to build, but gradually the walls rose and rose around her, until they towered clear above her head. Since they were all slippery with smoothness, she had no hope of ever being able to climb over them back into the road home, if indeed there was any longer such a road anywhere outside. Her heart sank within her, and she could scarcely hold up her head. To top it all, a glass house, which contained no trace of a cupboard, clearly did not contain a pantry. Flora began to feel sick with hunger and thirst, and to look forward in despair to no breakfast to-morrow.

Their houses at length put up, and their work over, the young builders gazed around them and exchanged compliments. In this particular playground, whatever might be spoken anywhere within its limits could be heard clearly by everyone there.

"Look," cried Angles, pointing gleefully, "just look at Quills, as red as fire. Red doesn't become Quills. Quills' house would look a good deal better without Quills."

"Talk of becomingness," laughed Quills, angrily, "you're just the color of a sour gooseberry, Angles, and a greater fright than we've seen you yet. Look at him, Sticky, look while you have the chance," for Angles was turning his green back on the speaker.

But Sticky—no wonder, the blocks *she* had fingered stuck together!—Sticky was too busy making faces at Slime, while Slime returned grimace for grimace. Sticky's house was blue and turned her purple. Slime's house—a very shaking one, ready to fall to pieces at any moment, and without one moment's warning—Slime's house was amber-hued and made her look sickly yellow. The quarrelers worked each other up into a state of fury, and having got long past variety, now did nothing but screech over and over again: Slime: "You're a sweet beauty"—and Sticky: "You're another!"

Quarrels raged throughout the playground. The only silent tongue was Flora's.

Suddenly, Hooks, who had built a carved house opposite the Queen's bubbled palace (both buildings were pale amethyst-colored), caught sight of his neighbor, and clapping his hands, burst out into an insulting laugh.

"You're another!" shrieked the Queen. Her words were weak, but as she spoke she stooped and clutched—shook—hurled—the first stone.

"Oh, don't, don't, don't," sobbed Flora, clinging in a fit of terror, and with all her weight, to the Queen's arm.

That first stone was like the first hailstone of a storm. Soon stones flew in every direction and at every height. Stone clattered, glass shivered, moans and groans resounded on every side. It was like a battle of giants. Who would be champion among these jealous peers?

The Queen. All that had whistled through the air were mere pebbles and chips compared with one massive slab, which she now heaved up—poised—prepared to launch—

"Oh, don't, don't, don't," cried out Flora again, almost choking with sobs. But it was useless. The enormous stone spun on, widening a hole through the palace wall on its way to crush Hooks. Half mad with fear, Flora flung herself after it through the opening—

And in one moment the scene was changed. Silence from human voices and a pleasant coolness of approaching twilight surrounded her. High overhead a fleet of rosy gray clouds went sailing away from the west, and outstripping these, blackbirds on flapping wings flew home to their nests in the lofty elm trees, and cawed as they flew. A sudden gust of wind ran rustling through the laurel leaves. Such dear familiar sights and sounds told Flora that she was sitting safe within her home grounds. Yes, in the very yew-tree alley, with its forty trees in all, not one more, and with no mysterious door leading out of it into a hall of misery.

She hurried indoors. Her parents, with Alfred, Susan, and the five visitors, were just sitting down around the tea table, and nurse was leaving the drawing room in some clear worry.

Wagga wagged his tail, Muff came forward purring, and a laugh greeted Flora. "Do you know," cried George, "that you have been fast asleep ever so long in the yew walk, for I found you there? And now nurse is on her way to fetch you in, if you hadn't turned up."

Flora said not a word in answer, but sat down just as she was, with tumbled dress and hair, and a look in her little face that made it very sweet and charming. Before tea was over, she had nestled close to Anne and whispered how sorry she was to have been so cross.

And I think if she lives to be nine years old and give another birthday party, she is likely on that occasion to be even less like the birthday Queen of her troubled dream than was the Flora of eight years old.

TWELVE

A Lost Paradise

by Andrew Lang

from *The Lilac Fairy Book* (1910)

In the middle of a great forest there lived a long time ago a charcoal-burner and his wife. They were both young and handsome and strong, and when they got married, they thought work would never fail them. But bad times came, and they grew poorer and poorer, and the nights in which they went hungry to bed became more and more frequent.

Now one evening the king of that country was hunting near the charcoal-burner's hut. As he passed the door, he heard a sound of sobbing, and being a good-natured man he stopped to listen, thinking that perhaps he might be able to give some help.

"Were there ever two people so unhappy!" said a woman's

voice. "Here we are, ready to work like slaves the whole day long, and no work can we get. And it is all because of the curiosity of old mother Eve! If she had only been like me, who never wants to know anything, we should all have been as happy as kings today, with plenty to eat, and warm clothes to wear. Why—" but at this point a loud knock interrupted her cries.

"Who is there?" asked she.

"I!" replied somebody.

"And who is 'I'?"

"The king. Let me in."

Full of surprise, the woman jumped up and pulled the bar away from the door. As the king entered, he noticed that there was no furniture in the room at all, not even a chair, so he pretended to be in too great a hurry to see anything around him, and only said, "You must not let me disturb you. I have no time to stay, but you seemed to be in trouble. Tell me: are you very unhappy?"

"Oh, my lord, we can find no work and have eaten nothing for two days!" she answered. "Nothing remains for us but to die of hunger."

"No, no, you shan't do that," cried the king, "or if you do, it will be your own fault. You shall come with me into my palace, and you will feel as if you were in Paradise, I promise you. In return, I only ask one thing of you, that you shall obey my orders exactly."

The charcoal-burner and his wife both stared at him for a moment, as if they could hardly believe their ears; and, indeed, it was not to be wondered at! Then they found their tongues, and exclaimed together, "Oh, yes, yes, my lord! We will do everything you tell us. How could we be so ungrateful as to disobey you, when you are so kind?"

The king smiled, and his eyes twinkled. "Well, let us start at once," he said. "Lock your door, and put the key in your pocket."

The woman looked as if she thought this was needless, seeing it was quite, quite certain they would never come back. But she dared not say so, and did as the king told her.

After walking through the forest for a couple of miles, they all three reached the palace. By the king's orders servants led the charcoal-burner and his wife into rooms filled with beautiful things such as they had never even dreamed of. First they bathed in green marble baths where the water looked like the sea, and then they put on silken clothes that felt soft and pleasant.

When they were ready, one of the king's special servants entered, and took them into a small hall, where dinner was laid, and this pleased them better than anything else.

They were just about to sit down to the table when the king walked in.

"I hope you have been attended to properly," he said, "and that you will enjoy your dinner. My steward will take care you have all you want, and I wish you to do exactly as you please. Oh, by the way, there is one thing! You notice that soup tureen in the middle of the table? Well, be careful on no account to lift the lid. If once you take off the cover, there is an end of your good fortune." Then, bowing to his guests, he left the room.

"Did you hear what he said?" inquired the charcoal-burner in an awe-stricken voice. "We are to have what we want, and do what we please. Only we must not touch the soup tureen."

"No, of course we won't," answered the wife. "Why should we wish to? But all the same it is rather odd, and one can't help wondering what is inside."

For many days life went on like a beautiful dream to the charcoal-burner and his wife. Their beds were so comfortable, they could hardly make up their minds to get up. Their clothes were so lovely, they could scarcely bring themselves to take them off. Their dinners were so good that they found it very difficult to leave off eating. Then outside the palace were gardens filled with rare flowers and fruits and singing birds, or if they desired to go further, a golden coach, painted with wreaths of forget-me-nots and lined with blue satin, awaited their orders. Sometimes it happened that the king came to see them, and he smiled as he glanced at the man, who was getting rosier and plumper each day. But when his eyes rested on the woman, they took on a look which seemed to say "I knew it," though this neither the charcoal-burner nor his wife ever noticed.

"Why are you so silent?" asked the man one evening when dinner had passed before his wife had spoken one word. "A little while ago you used to be chattering all the day long, and now I have almost forgotten the sound of your voice."

"Oh, nothing. I did not feel like talking, that was all!" She stopped, and added carelessly after a pause, "Don't you ever wonder what is in that soup tureen?"

"No, never," replied the man. "It is no business of ours," and the conversation dropped once more, but as time went on, the woman spoke less and less, and seemed so wretched that her husband grew quite frightened about her. As to her food, she refused one thing after another.

"My dear wife," said the man at last, "you really must eat something. What in the world is the matter with you? If you go on like this you will die."

"I would rather die than not know what is in that tureen," she burst out so violently that the husband was quite startled.

"Is that it?" he cried. "Are you making yourself miserable because of that? Why, you know we would be turned out of the palace, and sent away to starve."

"Oh no, we wouldn't. The king is too good-natured. Of course he didn't mean a little thing like this! Besides, there is no need to lift the lid off altogether. Just raise one corner so that I may peep. We are quite alone. Nobody will ever know."

The man hesitated: it did seem a "little thing," and if it was to make his wife contented and happy it was well worth the risk. So he took hold of the handle of the cover and raised it very slowly and carefully, while the woman stooped down to peep. Suddenly she jumped back with a scream, for a small mouse had sprung from the inside of the tureen, and had nearly hit her in the eye. Round and round the room it ran, round and round they both ran after it, knocking down chairs and vases in their efforts to catch the mouse and put it back in the tureen. In the middle of all the noise the door opened, and the mouse ran out between the feet of the king. In one instant both the man and his wife were hiding under the table, and to all appearances the room was empty.

"You may as well come out," said the king, "and hear what I have to say."

"I know what it is," answered the charcoal-burner, hanging his head. "The mouse has escaped."

"A guard of soldiers will take you back to your hut," said the king. "Your wife has the key."

"Weren't they silly?" cried the grandchildren of the charcoal-burner when they heard the story. "How we wish that we had had the chance! We should never have wanted to know what was in the soup tureen!"

THIRTEEN

Justnowland

by Edith Nesbit

from *The Magic World* (1912)

A untie! No, no, no! I will be good. Oh, I will!" The little weak voice came from the other side of the locked attic door.

"You should have thought of that before," said the strong, sharp voice outside.

"I didn't mean to be naughty. I didn't, truly."

"It's not what you mean, miss, it's what you do. I'll teach you not to mean, my lady."

The bitter irony of the last words dried the child's tears. "Very well, then," she screamed, "I won't be good. I won't try to be good. I thought you'd like your nasty old garden weeded. I only did it to please you. How was I to know it was turnips?

It looked just like weeds." Then came a pause, then another shriek. "Oh, Auntie, don't! Oh, let me out—let me out!"

"I'll not let you out until I've broken your spirit, my girl. You may depend on that."

The sharp voice stopped abruptly on a high note. Determined feet in strong boots sounded on the stairs—fainter, fainter. A door slammed below with a dreadful definiteness, and Elsie was left alone, to wonder how soon her spirit would break—for at no less a price, it appeared, could freedom be bought.

The outlook seemed hopeless. The martyrs and heroines, with whom Elsie usually identified herself—*their* spirits had never been broken. Not chains nor the rack nor the fiery stake itself had even weakened them. Imprisonment in an attic would have been luxury to them compared with the boiling oil and the smoking faggots and all the cruelties of mysterious instruments of steel and leather, in cold dungeons, lit only by the dull flare of torches and the bright, watchful eyes of inquisitors.

A month in the house of "Auntie" (really only an unrelated Mrs. Staines, paid to take care of the child) had held but one interest—Foxe's *Book of Martyrs*. It was a horrible book—the thick oleographs, their guarding sheets of tissue paper sticking to the prints like bandages to a wound. . . . Elsie knew all about wounds: she had had one herself. Only a burned hand, it is true, but a wound is a wound, all the world over. It was a book that made you afraid to go to bed, but it was a book you could not help reading. And now it seemed as though it might at last help, and not merely sicken and terrify. But the help was frail, and broke almost instantly on the thought—*They were brave because they were good. How can I be brave when there's nothing to be brave about except me not knowing the difference between turnips and weeds?*

She sank down, a huddled black bunch on the bare attic floor, and called wildly to someone who could not answer her. Her dress was black because the one who always used to answer could not answer any more. And her father was in India, where you cannot answer, or even hear, your little girl, however much she cries in England.

"I won't cry," said Elsie, sobbing as violently as ever. "I can be brave, even if I'm not a saint but only a turnip-mistaker. I'll be a Bastille prisoner, and tame a mouse!" She dried her eyes, though the bosom of the black frock still heaved like the sea after a storm, and looked about for a mouse to tame. One could not begin too soon. But unfortunately there seemed to be no mouse at liberty just then. There were mouse-holes right enough, all round the paneled walls, and in the broad, timeworn boards of the old floor. But never a mouse.

"Mouse, mouse!" Elsie called softly. "Mousie, mousie, come and be tamed!"

Not a mouse replied.

The attic was perfectly empty and dreadfully clean. The

other attic, Elsie knew, had lots of interesting things in it—old furniture and saddles, and sacks of seed potatoes—but in this attic, nothing. Not so much as a bit of string on the floor that one could make knots in, or twist round one's finger until it made the red ridges that are so interesting to look at afterwards; not even a piece of paper in the drafty, cold fireplace that one could make paper boats of, or prick letters in with a pin or the tag of one's shoelaces.

As she stooped to see whether under the grate some old matchbox or bit of twig might have escaped the broom, she saw suddenly what she had wanted most—a mouse. It was lying on its side. She put out her hand very slowly and gently, and whispered in her softest tones, "Wake up, Mousie, wake up, and come and be tamed." But the mouse never moved. And when she took it in her hand it was cold.

"Oh," she moaned, "you're dead, and now I can never tame you." She sat on the cold hearth and cried again, with the dead mouse in her lap.

"Don't cry," said somebody. "I'll find you something to tame—if you really want it."

Startled, Elsie saw the head of a black bird peering at her through the square opening that leads to the chimney. The edges of him looked ragged and rainbow-colored, but that was because she saw him through tears. To a tearless eye he was black and very smooth and sleek.

"Oh!" she said, and nothing more.

"Quite so," said the bird politely. "You are surprised to hear me speak, but your surprise will be, of course, much less when I tell you that I am really a Prime Minister condemned by an Enchanter to wear the form of a crow till . . . till I can get rid of it."

"Oh!"said Elsie.

"Yes, indeed," said the Crow, and suddenly grew smaller until he could come comfortably through the square opening. He did this, perched on the top bar, and hopped to the floor. And there he got bigger and bigger, and bigger and bigger and bigger. Elsie had scrambled to her feet, and then a little girl of eight and of the usual size stood face to face with a crow as big as a man, and no doubt as old. She found words then.

"Oh, don't!" she cried. "Don't get any bigger. I can't bear it."

"*I* can't *do* it," said the Crow kindly, "so that's all right. I thought you'd better get used to seeing rather large crows before I take you to Crownowland. We are all life-size there."

"But a crow's life-size isn't a man's life-size," Elsie managed to say.

"Oh, yes, it is—when it's an enchanted Crow," the bird replied. "That makes all the difference. Now you were saying you wanted to tame something. If you'll come with me to Crownowland I'll show you something worth taming."

"Is Crow-what's-its-name a nice place?" Elsie asked cautiously. She was, somehow, not so very frightened now.

"Very," said the Crow.

"Then perhaps I shall like it so much I shan't want to be taming things."

"Oh, yes, you will, when you know how much depends on it."

"But I shouldn't like," said Elsie, "to go up the chimney. This isn't my best dress, of course, but still. . . ."

"Quite so," said the Crow. "I only came that way for fun, and because I can fly. You shall go in by the chief gate of the kingdom, like a lady. Do come."

But Elsie still hesitated. "What sort of thing is it you want me to tame?" she said doubtfully.

The enormous crow hesitated. "A—a sort of lizard," it said at last. "And if you can only tame it so that it will do what you tell it to, you'll save the whole kingdom, and we'll put up a statue to you; but not in the People's Park, unless they wish it," the bird added mysteriously.

"I should like to save a kingdom," said Elsie, "and I like lizards. I've seen lots of them in India."

"Then you'll come?" said the Crow.

"Yes. But how do we go?"

"There are only two doors out of this world into another," said the Crow. "I'll take you through the nearest. Allow me!" It put its wing around her so that her face nestled against the black softness of the under-wing feathers. It was warm and dark and sleepy there, and very comfortable. For a moment she seemed to swim easily in a soft sea of dreams. Then, with a little shock, she found herself standing on a marble terrace, looking out over a city far more beautiful and wonderful than she had ever seen or imagined. The great man-sized Crow was by her side.

"Now," it said, pointing with the longest of its long black wing-feathers, "you see this beautiful city?"

"Yes," said Elsie, "of course I do."

"Well . . . I hardly like to tell you the story," said the Crow, "but it's a long time ago, and I hope you won't think the worse of us because we're really very sorry."

"If you're really sorry," said Elsie primly, "of course it's all right."

"Unfortunately it isn't," said the Crow. "You see the great square down there?"

Elsie looked down on a square of green trees, broken a little towards the middle.

"Well, that's where the . . . where it is—what you've got to tame, you know."

"But what did you do that was wrong?"

"We were unkind," said the Crow slowly, "and unjust, and ungenerous. We had servants and workpeople doing everything for us. We had nothing to do *but* be kind. And we weren't."

"Dear me," said Elsie feebly.

"We had several warnings," said the Crow. "There was an

old parchment, and it said just how you ought to behave and all that. But we didn't care what it said. I was Court Magician as well as Prime Minister, and I ought to have known better, but I didn't. We all wore frock-coats and high hats then," he added sadly.

"Go on," said Elsie, her eyes wandering from one beautiful building to another of the many that nestled among the trees of the city.

"And the old parchment said that if we didn't behave well our bodies would grow like our souls. But we didn't think so. And then all in a minute they *did*—and we were crows."

"But what was the dreadful thing you'd done?"

"We'd been unkind to the people who worked for us—not given them enough food or clothes or fire, and at last we took away even their play. There was a big park that the people played in, and we built a wall round it and took it for ourselves, and the King was going to set a statue of himself up in the middle. And then before we could begin to enjoy it we were turned into big crows; and the working people into big pigeons—and they can go where they like, but we have to stay here till we've tamed the. . . . We never can go into the park, until we've settled the thing that guards it. And that thing's a big, big lizard—in fact . . . it's a *dragon!*"

"*Oh!*" cried Elsie, but she was not as frightened as the Crow seemed to expect. Because every now and then she had felt sure that she was really safe in her own bed, and that this was a dream. It was not a dream, but the belief that it was made her very brave, and she felt quite sure that she could settle a dragon, if necessary—a dream dragon, that is. And the rest of the time she thought about Foxe's *Book of Martyrs* and what a heroine she now had the chance to be.

"You want me to kill it?" she asked.

"Oh no! To tame it," said the Crow. "We've tried all sorts of means—long whips, like people tame horses with, and red-hot bars, such as lion-tamers use—and it's all been perfectly useless; and there the dragon lives, and will live till someone can tame him and get him to follow them like a tame fawn, and eat out of their hand."

"What does the dragon like to eat?" Elsie asked.

"*Crows*," replied the other in an uncomfortable whisper. "At least *I've* never known it to eat anything else!"

"Am I to try to tame it now?" Elsie asked.

"Oh, dear, no," said the Crow. "We'll have a banquet in your honor, and you shall have tea with the Princess."

"How do you know who is a princess and who's not, if you're all crows?" Elsie cried.

"How do you know one human being from another?" the Crow replied. "Besides . . . Come on to the Palace."

It led her along the terrace, and down some marble steps to a small arched door. "The tradesmen's entrance," it explained. "Excuse it—the courtiers are crowding in by the front door." Then through long corridors and passages they went, and at last into the throne-room. Many crows stood about in respectful attitudes. On the golden throne, leaning a gloomy head upon the first joint of his right wing, the Sovereign of Crownowland was musing sadly. A little girl of about Elsie's age sat on the steps of the throne nursing a handsome doll.

"Who is the little girl?" Elsie asked.

"*Curtsey!* That's the Princess," the Prime Minister Crow whispered. Elsie made the best curtsey she could think of in such a hurry. "She wasn't wicked enough to be turned into a crow, or poor enough to be turned into a pigeon, so she remains a dear little girl, just as she always was."

The Princess dropped her doll and ran down the steps of the throne to meet Elsie.

"You dear!" she said. "You've come to play with me, haven't you? All the little girls I used to play with have turned into crows, and their beaks are so awkward at doll's tea-parties, and wings are no good to nurse dollies with. Let's have a doll's tea-party now, shall we?"

"May we?" Elsie looked at the Crow King, who nodded his head hopelessly. So, hand in hand, they went.

I wonder whether you have ever had the run of a perfectly beautiful palace and a nursery absolutely crammed with all the toys you ever had or wanted to have: dolls' houses, dolls' china tea sets, rocking horses, blocks, paint-boxes, magic tricks, pewter dinner-services, and any number of dolls. If you have, you may perhaps be able to imagine Elsie's happiness.

And better than all the toys was the Princess Perdona—so gentle and kind and jolly, full of ideas for games, and surrounded by the means for playing them. Think of it, after that bare attic, with not even a bit of string to play with, and no company but the poor little dead mouse!

There is no room in this story to tell you of all the games they had. I can only say that the time went by so quickly that they never noticed it going, and were amazed when the Crown nursemaid brought in the royal tea tray. Tea was a beautiful meal—with pink iced cake in it.

Now, all the time that these glorious games had been going on, and this magnificent tea, the wisest crows of Crownowland had been holding a council. They had decided that there was no time like the present, and that Elsie had better try to tame the dragon soon as late. "But," the King said, "she mustn't run any risks. A guard of fifty brave crows must go with her, and if the dragon shows the least temper, fifty crows must throw themselves between her and danger, even if it cost fifty-one crow-lives. I myself will lead that band. Who will volunteer?"

Volunteers, to the number of some thousands, instantly stepped forward, and the Field Marshal selected fifty of the strongest crows.

Then, in the pleasant pinkness of the sunset, Elsie was led out on to the palace steps, where the King made a speech and said what a heroine she was, and how like Joan of Arc. And the crows who had gathered from all parts of the town cheered madly. Did you ever hear crows cheering? It is a wonderful sound.

Then Elsie got into a magnificent golden coach, drawn by eight white horses, with a crow at the head of each horse. The Princess sat with her on the blue velvet cushions and held her hand.

"I know you'll do it," said she, "you're so brave and clever, Elsie!"

And Elsie felt braver than before, although now it did not seem so like a dream. But she thought of the martyrs, and held Perdona's hand very tight.

At the gates of the green park the Princess kissed and hugged her new friend. Her crown, which she had put on in honor of the occasion, got pushed quite on one side in the warmth of her embrace. Then Elsie stepped out of the carriage. There was a great crowd of crows round the park gates, and everyone cheered and shouted "Speech, speech!"

Elsie got as far as "Ladies and gentlemen—Crows, I mean," and then she could not think of anything more, so she simply added, "Please, I'm ready."

I wish you could have heard those crows cheer.

But Elsie wouldn't accept the crow guards.

"It's very kind," she said, "but the dragon only eats crows, and I'm not a crow, thank goodness—I mean, I'm not a crow—and if I've got to be brave I'd like to be brave, and none of you to get eaten. If only someone will come with me to show me the way and then run back as hard as he can when we get near the dragon. *Please!*"

"If only one goes *I* shall be the one," said the King. And he and Elsie went through the great gates side by side. She held the end of his wing, which was the nearest they could get to hand in hand.

The crowd outside waited in breathless silence. Elsie and the King went on through the winding paths of the People's Park. And by the winding paths they came at last to the dragon. He lay very peacefully on a great stone slab, his enormous bat-like wings spread out on the grass and his goldy-green scales glittering in the pretty pink sunset light.

"Go back!" said Elsie.

"No," said the King.

"If you don't," said Elsie, "*I* won't go *on*. Seeing a crow might make him furious, or give him an appetite, or something. Do—do go!"

So he went, but not far. He hid behind a tree, and from its shelter he watched.

Elsie drew a long breath. Her heart was thumping under the black frock. *Suppose*, she thought, *he mistakes me for a crow!* But she thought how yellow her hair was, and decided that the dragon would be certain to notice that.

"Quick march!" she said to herself. "Remember Joan of Arc," and walked right up to the dragon. It never moved, but watched her suspiciously out of its bright green eyes.

"Dragon dear!" she said in her clear little voice.

"*Eh?*" said the dragon, in tones of extreme astonishment.

"Dragon dear," she repeated, "do you like sugar?"

"*Yes,*" said the dragon.

"Well, I've brought you some. You won't hurt me if I bring it to you?"

The dragon violently shook its vast head.

"It's not much," said Elsie, "but I saved it at tea time. Four lumps. Two for each of my mugs of milk."

She laid the sugar on the stone slab by the dragon's paw.

It turned its head towards the sugar. The pinky sunset light fell on its face, and Elsie saw that it was weeping! Great fat tears as big as prize pears were running down its wrinkled cheeks.

"Oh, don't," said Elsie, "*don't* cry! Poor dragon, what's the matter?"

"Oh!" sobbed the dragon, "I'm only so glad you've come. I—I've been so lonely. No one to love me. You *do* love me, don't you?"

"I—I'm sure I shall when I know you better," said Elsie kindly.

"Give me a kiss, dear," said the dragon, sniffing.

It is no joke to kiss a dragon. But Elsie did it—somewhere on the hard green wrinkles of its forehead.

"Oh, thank you," said the dragon, brushing away its tears with the tip of its tail. "That breaks the charm. I can move now. And I've got back all my lost wisdom. Come along—I do want my tea!"

So, to the waiting crowd at the gate came Elsie and the dragon side by side. And at sight of the dragon, tamed, a great shout went up from the crowd, and at that shout each one in the crowd turned quickly to the next one—for it was the shout of men, and not of crows. At the first sight of the dragon, tamed, they had left off being crows forever and ever, and once again were men.

The King came running through the gates, his royal robes held high, so that he shouldn't trip over them, and he too was no longer a crow, but a man.

And what did Elsie feel after being so brave? Well, she felt that she would like to cry, and also to laugh, and she felt that she loved not only the dragon, but every man, woman, and child in the whole world—even Mrs. Staines.

She rode back to the Palace on the dragon's back.

And as they went the crowd of citizens who had been crows met the crowd of citizens who had been pigeons, and these were poor men in poor clothes.

It would have done you good to see how the ones who had been rich and crows ran to meet the ones who had been pigeons and poor.

"Come and stay at my house, brother," they cried to those who had no homes. "Brother, I have many coats; come and choose some," they cried to the ragged. "Come and feast with me!" they cried to all. And the rich and the poor went off arm in arm to feast and be glad that night, and the next day to work side by side. "For," said the King, speaking with his hand on the neck of the tamed dragon, "our land has been called Crownowland. But we are no longer crows. We are men: and we will be honorable men. And our country shall be called Justnowland forever and ever. And for the future we shall not be rich and poor, but fellow-workers, and each will do his best for his brothers and his own city. And your King shall be your servant!"

I don't know how they managed this, but no one seemed to think that there would be any difficulty about it when the King mentioned it; and when people really make up their minds to do anything, difficulties do most oddly disappear.

Wonderful rejoicings there were. The city was hung with flags and lamps. Bands played—the performers a little out of practice, because, of course, crows can't play the flute or the violin or the trombone—but the effect was very merry in-deed. Then came the time—it was quite dark—when the King rose up on his throne and spoke, and Elsie, among all her new friends, listened with them to his words.

"Our deliverer Elsie," he said, "was brought here by our Prime Minister. She has removed the enchantment that held us; and the dragon, now that he has had his tea and recov-ered from the shock of being kindly treated, turns out to be the second strongest magician in the world, and he will help us and advise us, so long as we remember that we are all brothers and fellow-workers. And now comes the time when our Elsie must return to her own place, or another go in her place. But we cannot send back our heroine, our deliverer." (*Long, loud cheering.*) "So one shall take her place. My daughter—"

The end of the sentence was lost in shouts of admiration. But Elsie stood up, small and white in her black frock, and said, "No, thank you. Perdona would simply hate it. And she doesn't know my daddy. He'll fetch me away from Mrs. Staines someday. . . ."

The thought of her daddy, far away in India, of the loneliness of Willow Farm, where now it would be night in that horrible bare attic where the poor dead little mouse was, nearly choked Elsie. It was so bright and light and good and kind here. And India was so far away. Her voice stayed a moment on a broken note.

"I—I. . . ." Then she spoke firmly.

"Thank you all so much," she said, "so very much. I do love you all, and it's lovely here. But, please, I'd like to go home now."

The Prime Minister, in a silence full of love and understanding, folded his dark cloak round her.

It was dark in the attic. Elsie, crouching alone in the blackness by the fireplace where the dead mouse had been, put out her hand to touch its cold fur.

There were wheels on the gravel outside—the knocker

swung strongly—*Rat*-tat-tat-tat-*Tat! Tat!*" A pause—voices—hasty feet in strong boots sounded on the stairs, the key turned in the lock. The door opened a dazzling crack, then fully, to the glare of a lamp carried by Mrs. Staines.

"Come down at once. I'm sure you're good now," she said, in a great hurry and in a new sweet voice.

But there were other feet on the stairs—a step that Elsie knew. "Where's my girl?" the voice she knew cried cheerfully. But under the cheerfulness Elsie heard something other and dearer. "Where's my girl?"

After all, it takes less than a month to come from India to the house in England where one's heart is.

Out of the bare attic and the darkness Elsie leaped into light, into arms she knew. "Oh, my daddy, my daddy!" she cried. "How glad I am I came back!"

PART FIVE

Nature's Wonders

The Mole was bewitched, entranced, fascinated. By the side of the river he trotted as one trots, when very small, by the side of a man who holds one spellbound by exciting stories; and when tired at last, he sat on the bank, while the river still chattered on to him, a babbling procession of the best stories in the world, sent from the heart of the earth to be told at last to the insatiable sea.

—Kenneth Grahame, *The Wind in the Willows*

FOURTEEN

The Conceited Apple-Branch

by Hans Christian Andersen

(written in 1852; translated into English in 1872)

It was the month of May. The wind still blew cold, but from bush and tree, field and flower, came the welcome sound, "Spring is come." Wildflowers in abundance covered the hedges. Under the little apple tree, Spring seemed busy, and told his tale from one of the branches which hung fresh and blooming, and covered with delicate pink blossoms that were just ready to open.

The branch well knew how beautiful it was. (This knowledge exists as much in the leaf as in the blood.) I was, therefore, not surprised when a nobleman's carriage, in which sat the young countess, stopped in the road nearby. She said that an apple-branch was a most lovely object, and an emblem of spring in its most charming aspect. Then the branch was broken off for her, and she held it in her delicate hand, and sheltered it with her silk parasol.

They drove to the castle, in which were lofty halls and splendid sitting rooms. Pure white curtains fluttered before the open windows. Beautiful flowers stood in shining, transparent vases. In one of them, which looked as if it had been cut out of newly fallen snow, the apple branch was placed, among some fresh, light twigs of beech. It was a charming sight.

Then the branch became proud, which was very much like human nature. People of every description entered the room, and, according to their position in society, they expressed their admiration. A few said nothing, others spoke too much, and the apple branch very soon got to understand that there was as much difference in the characters of human beings as in those of plants and flowers. Some are all for pomp and parade, others have a great deal to do to maintain their own importance, while the rest might be spared without much loss to society. So thought the apple branch, as he stood before the open window, from which he could see out over gardens and fields. There were flowers and plants enough for him to think and reflect upon—some rich and beautiful, some poor and humble indeed.

"Poor, despised herbs," said the apple branch. "There is really a difference between them and such as I am. How unhappy they must be, if they can feel as those in my position do! There is a difference indeed, and so there ought to be, or we should all be equals." And the apple branch looked with a sort of pity upon them, especially on a certain little flower that is found in fields and in ditches.

No one gathered these flowers together in a nosegay. They were too common. They were even known to grow between the paving stones, shooting up everywhere, like bad weeds. They bore the very ugly name of "dog-flowers" or "dandelions."

"Poor, despised plants," said the apple bough, "it is not your fault that you are so ugly, and that you have such an ugly name. But it is with plants as with men: there must be a difference."

"A difference!" cried the sunbeam, as he kissed the blooming apple branch, and then kissed the yellow dandelion out in the fields. All were brothers, and the sunbeam kissed them—the poor flowers as well as the rich. The apple bough had never thought of the boundless love of God, which reaches over all the works of creation, over everything which lives, and moves, and has its being in Him. He had never thought of the good and beautiful which are so often hidden, but can never remain forgotten by Him—not only among the lower creation, but also among men. The sunbeam, the ray of light, knew better. "You do not see very far, nor very clearly," he said to the apple branch. "Which is the despised plant you so specially pity?"

"The dandelion," he replied. "No one ever places it in a nosegay. It is often crushed under foot, there are so many of them. And when they run to seed, they have flowers like wool, which fly away in little pieces over the roads, and cling to the dresses of the people. They are only weeds, but of course there must be weeds. Oh, I am really very thankful that I was not made like one of these flowers."

Soon a whole group of children came across the fields. The youngest was so small that he had to be carried by the others. When he was seated on the grass, among the yellow flowers, he laughed aloud with joy, kicked out his little legs, rolled about, plucked the yellow flowers, and kissed them in child-like innocence. The older children broke off the flowers with long stems, bent the stalks one round the other, to form links, and made first a chain for the neck, then one to go across the shoulders, and hang down to the waist, and at last a wreath to wear around the head. They looked quite splendid in their garlands of green stems and golden flowers.

Then the oldest among them gathered carefully the faded flowers, on the stem of which was grouped together the seed, in the form of a white feathery crown. These loose, airy wool-flowers are very beautiful, and look like fine snowy feathers or down. The children held them to their mouths, and tried to blow away the whole crown with one puff of the breath. Their grandmothers had told them that whoever did so would be sure to have new clothes before the end of the year.

"Do you see," said the sunbeam, "do you see the beauty of these flowers? Do you see their powers of giving pleasure?"

"Yes, to children," said the apple bough.

By and by an old woman came into the field. With a blunt knife without a handle, she began to dig around the roots of some of the dandelion plants and pull them up. With some of these she intended to make tea for herself. The rest she was going to sell to the chemist, and get some money.

"But beauty is of higher value than all this," said the apple tree branch. "Only the chosen ones can be allowed into the realms of the beautiful. There is a difference between plants, just as there is a difference between men."

Then the sunbeam spoke of the boundless love of God, as seen in creation, and over all that lives, and of the equal giving of His gifts, both in time and in eternity.

"That is your opinion," said the apple bough.

Then some people came into the room, and, among them, the young countess, the lady who had placed the apple bough in the transparent vase, so pleasantly beneath the rays of the sunlight. She carried in her hand something that seemed like a flower. The object was hidden by two or three great leaves, which covered it like a shield, so that no draft or gust of wind could injure it. It was carried more carefully than the apple branch had ever been. Very cautiously the large leaves were removed, and there appeared the feathery seed-crown of the despised dandelion. This was what the lady had so carefully plucked, and carried home so safely covered, so that not one of its delicate feathery arrows should flutter away. She now drew it into view quite uninjured, and wondered at its beautiful form, and airy lightness, and extraordinary construction, so soon to be blown away by the wind.

"See," she exclaimed, "how wonderfully God has made this little flower. I will paint it with the apple branch together. Everyone admires the beauty of the apple bough, but this humble flower has been gifted by Heaven with another kind of loveliness. Although they differ in appearance, both are the children of the realms of beauty."

Then the sunbeam kissed the lowly flower, and he kissed the blooming apple branch, upon whose leaves appeared a rosy blush.

FIFTEEN
A Handful of Clay

by Henry Van Dyke

from *The Blue Flower* (1902)

There was a handful of clay in the bank of a river. It was only common clay, coarse and heavy; but it had high thoughts of its own value, and wonderful dreams of the great place which it was to fill in the world when the time came for its virtues to be discovered.

Overhead, in the spring sunshine, the trees whispered together of the glory which descended upon them when the delicate blossoms and leaves began to expand. The forest glowed with fair, clear colors, as if the dust of thousands of rubies and emeralds were hanging, in soft clouds, above the earth.

The flowers, surprised with the joy of beauty, bent their

heads to one another, as the wind caressed them, and said, "Sisters, how lovely you have become. You make the day bright."

The river, glad of new strength and rejoicing in the unison of all its waters, murmured to the shores in music, telling of its release from icy chains, its swift flight from the snow-clad mountains, and the mighty work to which it was hurrying—the wheels of many mills to be turned, and great ships to be floated to the sea.

Waiting blindly in its bed, the clay comforted itself with lofty hopes. "My time will come," it said. "I was not made to be hidden forever. Glory and beauty and honor are coming to me in due season."

One day the clay felt itself taken from the place where it had waited so long. A flat blade of iron passed beneath it, and lifted it, and tossed it into a cart with other lumps of clay. It was carried far away, as it seemed, over a rough and stony road. But it was not afraid, nor discouraged, for it said to itself, "This is necessary. The path to glory is always rugged. Now I am on my way to play a great part in the world."

But the hard journey was nothing compared with the pain and suffering that came after it. The clay was put into a trough and mixed and beaten and stirred and trampled. It seemed almost unbearable. But there was comfort in the thought that something very fine and noble was certainly coming out of all this trouble. The clay felt sure that, if it could only wait long enough, a wonderful reward was in store for it.

Then it was put upon a swiftly turning wheel, and whirled around until it seemed as if it must fly into a thousand pieces. A strange power pressed it and molded it, as it revolved. Through all the dizziness and pain, it felt that it was taking a new form.

Then an unknown hand put it into an oven, and fires were built around it—fierce and penetrating—hotter than all the heats of summer upon the bank of the river. Through it all, the clay held itself together and endured its trials, confident of a great future. *Surely*, it thought, *I am intended for something very splendid, since such effort is taken with me. Perhaps I am fashioned for the ornament of a temple, or a precious vase for the table of a king.*

At last the baking was finished. The clay was taken from the furnace and set down upon a board, in the cool air, under the blue sky. The tribulation was passed. The reward was at hand.

Close beside the board there was a pool of water, not very deep, nor very clear, but calm enough to reflect truly every image that fell upon it. There, for the first time, as it was lifted from the board, the clay saw its new shape, the reward of all its patience and pain—a common flowerpot, straight and stiff, red and ugly. And then it felt that it was not meant for a king's house, nor for a palace of art, because it was made without glory or beauty or honor. It murmured against the unknown maker, saying, "Why have you made me like this?"

Many days it passed in sullen unhappiness. Then the clay pot was filled with earth, and something rough and brown and dead-looking was pushed into the middle of the earth and covered over. The clay rebelled at this new disgrace. "This is the worst of all that has happened to me, to be filled with dirt and rubbish. Surely I am a failure."

But then it was set in a greenhouse, where the sunlight fell warm upon it, and water was sprinkled over it. Day by day as it waited, a change began to come to it. Something was stirring within it—a new hope. Still it was ignorant, and knew not what the new hope meant.

One day the clay was lifted again from its place, and carried into a great church. Its dream was coming true after all. It had a fine part to play in the world. Glorious music flowed over it. It was surrounded with flowers. Still it could not understand. So it whispered to another vessel of clay, like itself, close beside it, "Why have they set me here? Why do all the people look toward us?" And the other vessel answered, "Do you not know? You are carrying a royal scepter of lilies. Their petals are white as snow, and the heart of them is like pure gold. The people look this way because the flower is the most wonderful in the world. And the root of it is in your heart."

Then the clay was content, and silently thanked its maker, because, though an earthen vessel, it held so great a treasure.

SIXTEEN

The Nightingale

by Hans Christian Andersen

as presented by Andrew Lang in *The Yellow Fairy Book* (1894)

In long-ago China, the Emperor's Palace was the most splendid in the world, made of priceless porcelain, but so brittle and delicate that you had to take great care how you touched it. In the garden were the most beautiful flowers, and on the loveliest of them silver bells were tied, which tinkled so that if you passed you could not help looking at the flowers. Everything in the Emperor's garden was arranged for the best appearance, and the garden was so large that even the gardener himself did not know where it ended. If you ever got beyond it, you came to a majestic forest with great trees and deep lakes in it. The forest sloped down to the sea, which was a clear blue. Large ships could sail under the branches of the trees, and in these trees there lived a Nightingale. She sang so beautifully that even the poor fisherman who had so much to do stood and listened when he came at night to cast his nets. "How beautiful it is!" he said, but he had to attend to his work, and forgot about the bird. But when she sang the next night and the fisherman came there again, he said the same thing, "How beautiful it is!"

From all the countries round came travelers to the Emperor's town, who were astonished at the Palace and the garden. But when they heard the Nightingale they all said, "This is the finest thing after all!"

The travelers told all about it when they went home, and great scholars wrote many books upon the town, the Palace, and the garden, but the Nightingale was praised the most. All the poets composed splendid verses on the Nightingale in the forest by the deep sea.

The books were circulated throughout the world, and some of them reached the Emperor. He sat in his golden chair, and read and read. He nodded his head every moment, for he liked reading the brilliant accounts of the town, the Palace, and the garden. "But the Nightingale is better than all," he saw written.

"What is that?" said the Emperor. "I don't know anything about the Nightingale! Is there such a bird in my empire, and so near as in my garden? I have never heard it! Imagine reading for the first time about it in a book!"

And he called his First Lord to him. He was so proud that if anyone of lower rank than his own ventured to speak to him or ask him anything, he would say nothing but "P!" and that does not mean anything.

"Here is a most remarkable bird which is called a Nightingale!" said the Emperor. "They say it is the most glorious thing in my kingdom. Why has no one ever said anything to me about it?"

"I have never before heard it mentioned!" said the First Lord. "I will look for it and find it!"

But where was it to be found? The First Lord ran up and down stairs, through the halls and corridors, but none of those he met had ever heard of the Nightingale. And the First Lord ran again to the Emperor, and told him that it must be an invention on the part of those who had written the books.

"Your Imperial Majesty cannot really believe all that is written! There are some inventions called the Black Art!"

"But the book in which I read this," said the Emperor, "is sent me by His Great Majesty the Emperor of Japan; so it cannot be untrue, and I will hear the Nightingale! She must be here this evening! She has my gracious permission to appear, and if she does not, the whole Court shall be trampled under foot after supper!"

"Tsing pe!" said the First Lord; and he ran up and down stairs, through the halls and corridors, and half the Court ran with him, for they did not want to be trampled under foot. Everyone was asking after the wonderful Nightingale which all the world knew of, except those at Court.

At last they met a poor little girl in the kitchen, who said, "Oh! I know the Nightingale well. How she sings! I have permission to carry the scraps over from the Court meals to my poor sick mother, and when I am going home at night, tired and weary, and rest for a little in the wood, then I hear the Nightingale singing! It brings tears to my eyes, and I feel as if my mother were kissing me!"

"Little kitchen maid!" said the First Lord, "I will give you a place in the kitchen, and you shall have permission to see the Emperor at dinner, if you can lead us to the Nightingale, for she is invited to come to Court this evening."

And so they all went into the wood where the Nightingale usually sang, and half the Court went too.

When they were on the way there they heard a cow mooing.

"Oh!" said the Courtiers, "now we have found her! What a wonderful power for such a small beast to have! I am sure we have heard her before!"

"No, that is a cow mooing!" said the little kitchen maid. "We are still a long way off!"

Then the frogs began to croak in the marsh. "Splendid!" said the Chinese chaplain. "Now we hear her. It sounds like a little church bell!"

"No, no, those are frogs!" said the little kitchen maid. "But I think we shall soon hear her now!"

Then the Nightingale began to sing.

"There she is!" cried the little girl. "Listen! She is sitting there!" And she pointed to a little dark-gray bird up in the branches.

"Is it possible!" said the First Lord. "I should never have thought it! How ordinary she looks! She must surely have lost her feathers because she sees so many important men round her!"

"Little Nightingale," called out the little kitchen maid, "our Gracious Emperor wants you to sing before him!"

"With the greatest of pleasure!" said the Nightingale; and she sang so gloriously that it was a pleasure to listen.

"It sounds like glass bells!" said the First Lord. "And look how her little throat works! It is wonderful that we have never heard her before! She will be a great success at Court."

"Shall I sing once more for the Emperor?" asked the Nightingale, thinking that the Emperor was there.

"My esteemed little Nightingale," said the First Lord, "I have the great pleasure to invite you to Court this evening, where His Gracious Imperial Highness will be enchanted with your charming song!"

"It sounds best in the green wood," said the Nightingale. But still, she came gladly when she heard that the Emperor wished it.

At the Palace everything was splendidly prepared. The porcelain walls and floors glittered in the light of many thousand gold lamps. The most gorgeous flowers were placed in the corridors. In the center of the great hall where the Emperor sat was a golden perch, on which the Nightingale sat. The whole Court was there, and the little kitchen maid was allowed to stand behind the door, now that she was a Court cook. Everyone was dressed in his best, and everyone was looking towards the little gray bird to whom the Emperor nodded.

The Nightingale sang so gloriously that tears came into the Emperor's eyes and ran down his cheeks. Then the Nightingale sang even more beautifully; it went straight to all hearts. The Emperor was so delighted that he said she should wear his gold slipper around her neck. But the Nightingale thanked him, and said she had had enough reward already. "I have seen tears in the Emperor's eyes—that is a great reward. An Emperor's tears have such power!" Then she sang again with her gloriously sweet voice.

"That is the most charming display I have ever seen!" said all the ladies round. And they all started to hold water in their mouths so they might gurgle whenever anyone spoke to them. Then they thought themselves nightingales. Yes, the lackeys and chambermaids announced that they were pleased; which means a great deal, for they are the most difficult people of all to satisfy. In short, the Nightingale was a real success.

She had to stay at Court now. She had her own cage, and permission to walk out twice in the day and once at night.

She was given twelve servants, who each held a silken string which was fastened round her leg. There was little pleasure in flying about like this.

The whole town was talking about the wonderful bird, and when two people met each other one would say "Nightin," and the other "Gale," and then they would both sigh and understand one another.

Yes, and eleven grocers' children were named after her, but not one of them could sing a note.

One day the Emperor received a large parcel on which was written "The Nightingale."

"Here is another new book about our famous bird!" said the Emperor.

But it was not a book. It was a little mechanical toy, which lay in a box—an artificial nightingale which was like the real one, only it was set all over with diamonds, rubies, and sapphires. When it was wound up, it could sing the piece the real bird sang, and moved its tail up and down, and glittered with silver and gold. Around its neck was a little collar on which was written, "The Nightingale of the Emperor of Japan is nothing compared to that of the Emperor of China."

"This is magnificent!" they all said, and the man who had brought the clockwork bird received on the spot the title of "Bringer of the Imperial First Nightingale."

"Now they must sing together. What a duet we shall have!"

And so they sang together, but their voices did not blend, for the real Nightingale sang in her way and the clockwork bird sang waltzes.

"It is not its fault!" said the bandmaster. "It keeps very good time and is quite my style!"

Then the artificial bird had to sing alone. It gave just as much pleasure as the real one, and then it was so much prettier to look at; it sparkled like bracelets and necklaces. Three-and-thirty times it sang the same piece without being tired. People would like to have heard it again, but the Emperor thought that the living Nightingale should sing now—but where was she? No one had noticed that she had flown out of the open window away to her green woods.

"What *shall* we do!" said the Emperor.

All the Court scolded, and said that the Nightingale was very ungrateful. "But we still have the best bird!" they said and the artificial bird had to sing again, and that was the thirty-fourth time they had heard the same piece. But they did not yet know it by heart; it was much too difficult. And the bandmaster praised the bird tremendously; yes, he assured them it was better than a real nightingale, not only because of its beautiful plumage and diamonds, but inside as well. "For see, my Lords and Ladies and your Imperial Majesty, with the real Nightingale one can never tell what will come out, but all is known about the artificial bird! You can explain it, you can open it and show people where the waltzes lie, how they go, and how one follows the other!"

"That's just what we think!" said everyone in the Court. And the bandmaster received permission to show the bird to the people the next Sunday. When they heard it, they all said "Oh!" and held up their forefingers and nodded time. But the poor fishermen who had heard the real Nightingale said: "This one sings well enough, the tunes glide out; but there is something lacking—I don't know what!"

The real Nightingale was banished from the kingdom.

The artificial bird was put on silken cushions by the Emperor's bed. All the presents which it received, gold and precious stones, lay round it, and it was given the title of Imperial Night-singer, First from the Left. For the Emperor counted that side as the more distinguished, being the side on which the heart is.

And the bandmaster wrote a work of twenty-five volumes about the artificial bird. It was so learned, long, and so full of the hardest Chinese words that everyone said they had read it and understood it; for once they had been very stupid about a book, and had been trampled under foot as a result.

A whole year passed. The Emperor, the Court, and all the Chinese knew every note of the artificial bird's song by heart. But they liked it all the better for this; they could even sing with it, and they did. The street boys sang "Tra-la-la-la-la," and the Emperor sang too sometimes. It was indeed delightful.

But one evening, when the artificial bird was singing its best, and the Emperor lay in bed listening to it, something in the bird went crack. Something snapped! Whir-r-r! all the wheels ran down and then the music stopped. The Emperor sprang up, and had his physician called, but what could *he* do! Then the clockmaker came, and, after a great deal of talking and examining, he put the bird somewhat in order, but he said that it must be used very little since its works were nearly worn out, and it was impossible to put in new ones. Here was a disaster! Only once a year the artificial bird was allowed to sing, and even that was almost too much for it. But then the bandmaster made a little speech full of hard words, saying that it was just as good as before. And so, of course, it *was* just as good as before. So five years passed, and then a great sorrow came to the nation. The Chinese look upon their Emperor as everything, and now he was ill, and not likely to live it was said.

Already a new Emperor had been chosen, and the people stood outside in the street and asked the First Lord how the old Emperor was. "P!" he said, and shook his head.

Cold and pale lay the Emperor in his splendid great bed. The whole Court believed him dead, and one after the other left him to pay their respects to the new Emperor. Everywhere in the halls and corridors cloth was laid down so that no footstep could be heard, and everything was still—very, very still. And nothing came to break the silence.

The Emperor longed for something to come and relieve this deathlike stillness. If only someone would speak to him! If only someone would sing to him. Music would carry his thoughts away, and would break the spell lying on him. The moon was streaming in at the open window, but that, too, was silent, quite silent.

"Music! music!" cried the Emperor. "You little bright golden bird, sing! Do sing! I gave you gold and jewels. I have hung my gold slipper round your neck with my own hand—sing! Do sing!" But the bird was silent. There was no one to wind it up, and so it could not sing. And all was silent, so terribly silent!

All at once there came in at the window the most glorious burst of song. It was the little living Nightingale, who, sitting outside on a branch, had heard the need of her Emperor and had come to sing to him of comfort and hope. And as she sang the blood flowed quicker and quicker in the Emperor's weak limbs, and life began to return.

"Thank you, thank you!" said the Emperor. "You divine little bird! I know you. I chased you from my kingdom, and you have given me life again! How can I reward you?"

"You have done that already!" said the Nightingale. "I brought tears to your eyes the first time I sang. I shall never forget that. They are jewels that bring joy to a singer's heart. But now sleep and get strong again. I will sing you a lullaby." And the Emperor fell into a deep, calm sleep as she sang.

The sun was shining through the window when he awoke,

strong and well. None of his servants had come back yet, for they thought he was dead. But the Nightingale sat and sang to him.

"You must always stay with me!" said the Emperor. "You shall sing whenever you like, and I will break the artificial bird into a thousand pieces."

"Don't do that!" said the Nightingale. "He did his work as long as he could. Keep him as you have done! I cannot build my nest in the Palace and live here, but let me come whenever I like. I will sit in the evening on the bough outside the window, and I will sing you something that will make you feel happy and grateful. I will sing of joy, and of sorrow; I will sing of the evil and the good which lies hidden from you. The little singing bird flies all around, to the poor fisherman's hut, to the farmer's cottage, to all those who are far away from you and your Court. I love your heart more than your crown, though that has about it a brightness as of something holy. Now I will sing to you again, but you must promise me one thing—"

"Anything!" said the Emperor, standing up in his Imperial robes, which he had put on himself, and fastening on his sword richly decorated with gold.

"One thing I beg of you! Don't tell anyone that you have a little bird who tells you everything. It will be much better not to!" Then the Nightingale flew away.

The servants came in to look at their dead Emperor.

The Emperor said, "Good morning!"

PART SIX

HEAVENLY MARVELS

I saw Eternity the other night,
Like a great ring of pure and endless light,
All calm as it was bright.
—**Henry Vaughan**

SEVENTEEN

A Christmas Star

by Katherine Pyle

from *The Children's Book of Christmas Stories*
edited by Asa Don Dickinson and Ada M. Skinner (1913)

Come now, my dear little stars," said Mother Moon, "and I will tell you the Christmas story."

Every morning for a week before Christmas, Mother Moon used to call all the little stars around her and tell them a story.

It was always the same story, but the stars never grew tired of it. It was the story of the Christmas star—the Star of Bethlehem.

When Mother Moon had finished the story the little stars always said, "And the star is shining still, isn't it, Mother Moon, even if we can't see it?"

And Mother Moon would answer, "Yes, my dears, only now it shines for men's hearts instead of their eyes."

Then the stars would tell Mother Moon goodnight and put on their little blue nightcaps and go to bed in the sky chamber; for the stars' bedtime is when people down on the earth are beginning to waken and see that it is morning.

But that particular morning when the little stars said goodnight and went quietly away, one golden star still lingered beside Mother Moon.

"What is the matter, my little star?" asked Mother Moon. "Why don't you go with your little sisters?"

"Oh, Mother Moon," said the golden star. "I am so sad! I wish I could shine for someone's heart like that star of wonder that you tell us about."

"Why, aren't you happy up here in the sky country?" asked Mother Moon.

"Yes, I have been very happy," said the star, "but tonight it seems just as if I must find some heart to shine for."

"Then if that is so," said Mother Moon, "the time has come, my little star, for you to go through the Wonder Entry."

"The Wonder Entry? What is that?" asked the star. But Mother Moon made no answer.

Rising, she took the little star by the hand and led it to a door that it had never seen before.

Mother Moon opened the door, and there was a long dark entry. At the far end was shining a little speck of light.

"What is this?" asked the star.

"It is the Wonder Entry, and it is through this that you

must go to find the heart where you belong," said Mother Moon.

Then the little star was afraid.

It longed to go through the entry as it had never longed for anything before, and yet it was afraid and clung to Mother Moon.

But very gently, almost sadly, Mother Moon drew her hand away. "Go, my child," she said.

Then, wondering and trembling, the little star stepped into the Wonder Entry, and the door of the sky house closed behind it.

The next thing the star knew it was hanging in a toy shop with a whole row of other stars—blue and red and silver. It was gold. The shop smelled of evergreen, and was full of Christmas shoppers, men and women and children. Of them all, the star looked at no one but a little boy standing in front of the counter. As soon as the star saw the child, it knew that he was the one to whom it belonged.

The little boy was standing beside a sweet-faced woman and he was not looking at anything in particular.

The star shook and trembled on the string that held it for fear that the child would not see it, or if he did, he would not know it as his star.

The lady had a number of toys on the counter before her, and she was saying, "Now I think we have presents for everyone: There's the doll for Lou, and the game for Ned, and the music box for May; and then the rocking horse and the sled."

Suddenly the little boy caught her by the arm. "Oh, Mother," he said. He had seen the star.

"Well, what is it, darling?" asked the lady.

"Oh, Mother, just see that star up there! I wish—oh, I do wish I had it."

"My dear, we have so many things for the Christmas tree," said the mother.

"Yes, I know, but I do want the star," said the child.

"Very well," said the mother, smiling. "Then we will take that, too."

So the star was taken down from the place where it hung and wrapped up in a piece of paper. All the while it thrilled with joy, for now it belonged to the little boy.

It was not until the afternoon before Christmas, when the tree was being decorated, that the golden star was unwrapped and taken out from the paper.

"Here is something else," said the sweet-faced lady. "We must hang this on the tree. Paul took such a fancy to it that I had to get it for him. He will never be satisfied unless we hang it on too."

"Oh, yes," said someone else who was helping to decorate the tree. "We will hang it here on the very top."

So the little star hung on the highest branch of the Christmas tree.

That evening all the candles were lighted on the Christmas tree, and there were so many that they fairly dazzled the eyes. The gold and silver balls, the fairies and the glass fruits, shone and twinkled in the light. And high above them all shone the golden star.

At seven o'clock a bell was rung, and then the folding doors of the room where the Christmas tree stood were thrown open, and a crowd of children came trooping in.

They laughed and shouted and pointed, and all talked together. After a while there was music, and presents were taken from the tree and given to the children.

How different it all was from the great wide, still sky house!

But the star had never been so happy in all its life, for the little boy was there.

He stood apart from the other children, looking up at the star, with his hands clasped behind him, and he did not seem to care for the toys and the games.

At last it was all over. The lights were put out, the children went home, and the house grew still.

Then the ornaments on the tree began to talk among themselves.

"So that is all over," said a silver ball. "It was very merry this evening—the merriest Christmas I remember."

"Yes," said a glass bunch of grapes, "the best of it is over. Of course people will come to look at us for several days yet, but it won't be like this evening."

"And then I suppose we'll be put away for another year," said a paper fairy. "Really, it seems hardly worthwhile. Such a few days out of the year and then to be shut up in the dark box again. I almost wish I were a paper doll."

The bunch of grapes was wrong in saying that people would come to look at the Christmas tree the next few days. Instead, it stood neglected in the library and nobody came near it. Everybody in the house went about very quietly, with anxious faces because the little boy was ill.

At last, one evening, a woman came into the room with a servant. The woman wore the cap and apron of a nurse.

"That is it," she said, pointing to the golden star. The servant climbed up on some steps and took down the star and put it in the nurse's hand. She carried it out into the hall and upstairs to a room where the little boy lay.

The sweet-faced lady was sitting by the bed, and as the nurse came in she held out her hand for the star.

"Is this what you wanted, my darling?" she asked, bending over the little boy.

The child nodded and held out his hands for the star, and as he clasped it a wonderful, shining smile came over his face.

The next morning the little boy's room was very still and dark.

The golden piece of paper that had been the star lay on a table beside the bed, its five points very sharp and bright.

But it was not the real star, any more than a person's body is the real person.

The real star was living and shining now in the little boy's heart. It had gone out with him into a new and more beautiful sky country than it had ever known before—the sky country where heaven's children live, each one carrying in its heart its own particular star.

EIGHTEEN

The Coming of the King

by Laura E. Richards

from *The Golden Windows* (1908)

Some children were at play in their playground one day, when a messenger rode through the town, blowing a trumpet, and crying aloud, "The King! The King passes by this road today. Make ready for the King!"

The children stopped their play and looked at one another.

"Did you hear that?" they said. "The King is coming. He may look over the wall and see our playground; who knows? We must put it in order."

The playground was sadly dirty. In the corners were scraps of paper and broken toys, for these were careless children. But now, one brought a hoe, and another a rake, and a third ran to get the wheelbarrow from behind the garden gate. They worked hard, until finally all was clean and tidy.

"Now it is clean!" they said. "But we must make it pretty, too, for kings are used to fine things. Maybe he would not notice just cleanness, for he may have it all the time."

Then one brought sweet rushes and spread them on the ground. Others made garlands of oak leaves and pine tassels and hung them on the walls. The littlest one pulled marigold buds and threw them all about the playground, "to look like gold," he said.

When all was done the playground was so beautiful that the children stood and looked at it, and clapped their hands with pleasure.

"Let us keep it always like this!" said the littlest one. And the others cried, "Yes! Yes! That is what we will do."

They waited all day for the coming of the King, but he never came. Toward sunset, a man with travel-worn clothes, and a kind, tired face passed along the road. He stopped to look over the wall.

"What a pleasant place!" said the man. "May I come in and rest, dear children?"

The children brought him in gladly. They set him on the seat that they had made out of an old barrel. They had covered it with an old red cape to make it look like a throne, and it made a very good one.

"It is our playground!" they said. "We made it pretty for

the King, but he did not come, and now we mean to keep it so for ourselves."

"That is good!" said the man.

"Because we think pretty and clean is nicer than ugly and dirty!" said another.

"That is better!" said the man.

"And for tired people to rest in!" said the littlest one.

"That is best of all!" said the man.

He sat and rested, and looked at the children with such kind eyes that they came around him. They told him all they knew—about the five puppies in the barn, and the bird's nest with four blue eggs, and the shore where the gold shells grew. The man nodded and understood all about it.

By and by he asked for a cup of water, and they brought it to him in the best cup, with the gold sprigs on it. Then he thanked the children, and rose and went on his way. But before he went he laid his hand on their heads for a moment, and the touch went warm to their hearts.

The children stood by the wall and watched the man as he went slowly along. The sun was setting, and the light fell in long slanting rays across the road.

"He looks so tired!" said one of the children.

"But he was so kind!" said another. "See!" said the littlest one. "How the sun still shines on his hair! It looks like a crown of gold."

NINETEEN

The Castle

by George MacDonald

from *Adela Cathcart* (1864)

On the top of a high cliff, forming part of the base of a great mountain, stood a lofty castle. When or how it was built, no one knew. Everyone who looked upon it felt that it was lordly and noble, and where one part seemed not to fit with another, the wise and humble dared not to call them out of place, but presumed that the whole castle might be built on some higher standard of architecture than they yet understood. What helped them to this conclusion was that no one had ever seen the whole of the building. Even of the portion best known, some part or other was always wrapped in thick folds of mist from the mountain. When the sun shone upon this mist, the parts of the building that appeared through the mist seemed to belong to some heavenly house in the land of the sunset. Those who looked could hardly tell whether they had ever seen them before, or whether they were now for the first time partly revealed.

Although the castle was occupied, those who lived in it often discovered rooms they had never entered before—once or twice, whole suites of apartments, of which only dim legends had been handed down from olden times. Some of them expected to find, one day, secret places, filled with treasures of wondrous jewels; among which they hoped to see Solomon's ring. It had for ages disappeared from the earth, but it still controlled the spirits, and the possession of it made a man simply what a man should be, the king of the world. Now and then, a narrow, winding stair, up till then unclimbed, would bring them out on a new tower, where new views of the surrounding country spread out before them. How many more of these there might be, or how much higher, no one could tell. The foundations of the castle in the rock could not be uncovered with the least accuracy. Those of the family who had tried, found a maze of chambers and passages, and endless series of down-going stairs, out of one underground space into a yet lower. They came to the conclusion that the whole mountain was perforated and honeycombed in this way. They had a dim awareness, too, of the presence, in those awful regions, of beings whom they could not recognize. Once, they came upon the edge of a great black gulf, where the eye could see nothing but darkness. They shrank back with horror, for the conviction flashed upon them that the gulf went down into the very central spaces of the earth; that the seething blackness before them had mysterious connections with the far-off voids of space, into which the stars dare not enter.

At the foot of the cliff, where the castle stood, lay a deep lake. It was inaccessible except by a few paths, because it was surrounded on all sides with cliffs which made the water look very black, although it was pure as the night sky. From a door in the castle, which was not to be otherwise entered, a broad flight of steps, cut in the rock, went down to the lake, and disappeared below its surface. Some thought the steps went to the very bottom of the water.

Now in this castle there lived a large family of brothers and sisters. They had never seen their father or mother. The younger children had been educated by the older, and the older ones had received an unseen care and support, the source of which they had, somehow or other, thought about very little. What people are accustomed to, they look upon as coming from nobody; as if help and progress and joy and love were the natural crops of Chaos or old Night. But Tradition said that one day— it was utterly uncertain when—their father would come, and leave them no more; for he was still alive, though where he lived nobody knew. In the meantime, all the rest had to obey their oldest brother, and listen to his advice.

But almost all the family was very fond of liberty, as they called it. They liked to run up and down, hither and thither, roving about, with neither law nor order, just as they pleased. So they could not stand their brother's tyranny, as they called it. At one time they said that he was only one of them, and therefore they would not obey him. At another, they said that he was not like them, and could not understand them, and therefore they would not obey him. Yet, sometimes, when he came and looked them full in the face, they were terrified, and dared not disobey, for he was stately and stern and strong.

Not one of them loved him heartily, except the oldest sister, who was very beautiful and silent, and whose eyes shone as if light lay somewhere deep behind them. And although she loved him, she thought he was very hard sometimes. For when he had once said a thing plainly, he could not be persuaded to think it over again. So even she forgot him sometimes, and went her own ways, and enjoyed herself without him. Most of them viewed him as a sort of watchman, whose business it was to keep them in order, and so they were angry and disliked him. Yet they all had a secret feeling that they ought to be obedient to him, and after any particular act of disrespect, none of them could think, with any peace, of the old story about the return of their father to his house. But indeed they never thought much about it, or about their father at all; for how could those who cared so little for their brother, whom they saw every day, care for their father whom they had never seen?

One chief cause of complaint against their oldest brother was that he interfered with their favorite studies and activities. Actually, he only tried to make them give up fooling around with serious things. He wanted them to search for truth, and not for amusement, from the many wonders around them. He did not want them to turn to other studies, or to give up pleasures; but, in those studies, he wanted them to put the highest things first, and other things in proportion to their true worth and goodness. This was unpleasant to those who did not care for what was higher than they. And so matters went on for a time. They thought they could do better without their brother, and their brother knew they could not do at all without him, and tried to fulfill the duty placed into his hands.

Eventually, one day, they talked together about giving a great party in their grandest rooms for any of their neighbors who chose to come, or indeed to anyone who would visit them. They were too proud to consider that some company might poison even the dwellers in what was undoubtedly the finest palace on the face of the earth. But what made the thing worse was that the old tradition said that these rooms were to be kept entirely for the use of the owner of the castle. Indeed, whenever they entered them, the rooms' majesty and splendor made them think of the old story, and they could not help believing it. Their brother would not let them forget it now. He appeared suddenly among them, when they had no thought of being interrupted by him. He scolded them, both for the nature of their invitation, and for their intention to introduce anyone into the rooms reserved for the use of the unknown father. But by this time their talk with each other had so excited their expectation of enjoyment that anger sprang up within them at the thought of being deprived of their hopes.

They looked at each other and the look said, "We are many and he is one. Let us get rid of him, for he is always finding fault, and getting in the way of the most innocent pleasures— as if we would wish to do anything wrong!"

Without a word spoken, they rushed upon him. And although he was stronger than any of them, and struggled hard at first, they overcame him at last. Indeed, some of them thought he gave up long before they had defeated him, and his surrender terrified the more tenderhearted among them. However, they bound him and carried him down many stairs. Having remembered an iron fastener in the wall of a certain chamber, with a thick rusty chain attached to it, they carried him there, and made the chain secure around him. There they left him, shutting the great metal door of the vault, as they left for the upper part of the castle.

Now all was in an uproar of preparation. Everyone was talking of the coming party, but no one spoke of the deed they had done. A sudden paleness spread over the face, first of one, and then of another. But it passed away, and no one took any notice of it. They only pursued the task of the moment more strongly. Messengers were sent far and near, announcing in all the public places a general invitation to any who chose to come on a certain day, and share for several days the hospitality of the castle dwellers. Many preparations immediately began for accepting the invitation. But their best neighbors refused to appear; not from pride, but because of the improper and careless way the invitation was made. Some of them had a custom of only going to another's house when invited in person. Others, knowing what sort of people would be there, made up their minds at once not to go. Yet multitudes, many of them beautiful and innocent as well as merry, decided to attend.

Meanwhile, the great rooms of the castle were made ready—that is, they spoiled them with decorations. There was a seriousness and splendor about the rooms in their ordinary condition, which made the lighthearted company so soon to move about in them seem out of place.

One day, while the workmen were busy, the oldest sister happened to enter. Suddenly the great idea of the mighty halls dawned upon her and filled her soul. The so-called decorations vanished from her sight, and she felt as if she stood in her father's presence. She was at once lifted and humbled. Just as suddenly the idea faded, and she saw only the gaudy decorations and draperies and paintings which ruined the grandeur. She wept and ran away. She had not been present when her brother was imprisoned, and indeed for some days had been so wrapped up in her own business that she had paid little attention to anything that was going on. But they all expected her to show herself when the company was gathered, and they had come to her for advice at various times during their operations. Now it was too late to interfere, and things must take their course.

At last the expected hour came, and the company began to gather. It was a warm summer evening. The dark lake reflected the rose-colored clouds in the west, and many gaily painted boats with colored flags sailed toward the massy rock on which the castle stood. The trees and flowers seemed already asleep, and breathing out their sweet dream-breath. Laughter and low voices rose from the lake to the ears of the young men and maidens looking out from the lofty windows. They went down to the broad platform at the top of the stairs in front of the door to receive their visitors. Gradually the festivities of the evening began. The same smiles flew from eyes and lips, darting like beams through the gathering crowd. Music, from unseen sources, now rolled in billows, now crept in ripples through the sea of air that filled the rooms. And in the dancing halls, hand took hand, and form and motion were swayed by the music. The floors bent beneath the feet of the dancers. But twice in the evening some of the partygoers were startled, and their faces became pale, for they felt as if the floor rose slightly to answer their feet. And all the time their brother lay below in the dungeon. Outside, all around the castle, brooded the dark night. The clouds had come up from all sides and were crowding together overhead. The music seldom paused, but when it did they might have heard, now and then, the gusty rush of a lonely wind.

When the celebrations were at their peak, a sudden crash of thunder overwhelmed the music. The windows were pushed in, and torrents of rain, carried by a rushing wind, poured into the halls. The lights went out, and the great rooms, now dark within, were darkened yet more by the dazzling shoots of lightning from the sky overhead. Those who dared to look out of the windows saw, in the blue brilliancy of the quick jets of lightning, the lake at the foot of the rock. Ordinarily so still and so dark, it was lighted up, not on the surface only, but down to half its depth.

The mass of people who flowed with the music broke into individuals, and they stood drenched, cold, and numb, with clinging garments. And in every heart ruled the belief that this was the only reality, and the party was but a dream. The oldest sister stood with clasped hands and bowed head, shivering and speechless, as if waiting for something to follow. Soon a terrible flash and thunder-peal made the castle rock. In the silence that followed, she heard the rattling of a chain far off, deep down. Soon the sound of heavy footsteps, along with the clanking of iron, reached her ear. Even in the darkness and roaring storm, she knew that her oldest brother had entered the room. A moment later, a continuous pounding of angry blue light began. This lasted for some moments and showed him standing in their midst, thin, tired, and motionless; his hair and beard untrimmed, his face frightening, his eyes large and hollow. The light seemed to gather around him. Indeed, some believed that it throbbed and shone from his person, and not from the stormy heavens above them. The lightning had torn open the wall of his prison, and released the iron staple of his chain, which he had wound about him like a girdle. In his hand he carried an iron bar, which he had found on the floor of the chamber. More terrified at his appearance than at all the violence of the storm, the visitors, with many a shriek and cry, rushed out into the wild night. Little by little, the storm died away. Its last flash showed the brothers and sisters lying, with their faces on the floor, and that fearful shape standing motionless amid them still.

Morning dawned, and there they lay, and there he stood. But at a word from him, they arose and went slowly about their various duties. The oldest sister was the last to rise, and when she did, it was only by a great effort that she reached her room, where she fell again on the floor. There she remained lying for days. The brother ordered the doors of the great rooms to be closed, leaving them just as they were, with all the childish decorations scattered about, and the rain still falling in through the shattered windows. "Thus let them lie," he said, "until the rain and frost have cleaned them of paint and drapery. No storm can hurt the pillars and arches of these halls."

The hours of this day went heavily. The storm was gone, but the rain was left. Dull and dark, the low misty clouds brooded over the castle and the lake, and shut out all the neighborhood. Even if they had climbed to the highest tower they knew, they would have found it covered in a garment of clinging mist. There was one lofty tower that rose a hundred feet above the rest, and from which the fog could have been seen lying in a gray mass beneath; but that tower they had not yet discovered, nor another close beside it, the top of which was never seen, nor could be, for the highest clouds of heaven clustered constantly around it. Outside the rain fell continuously, though not heavily; and inside, too, there were clouds from which dropped tears, which are the rain of the spirit. All the good of life seemed to have left, and their hearts were like leafless trees that had forgotten the joy of the summer. They moved about mechanically, and did not have strength enough left to wish to die.

The next day the clouds were higher, and a little wind blew through holes in the towers not yet filled with glass. Throughout the day, the brother gave gentle commands, first to one and then to another of his family. He was obeyed in silence. The wind blew fresher through the shattered windows of the great rooms, and found its way to faces and eyes hot with weeping. It cooled and blessed them. When the sun arose the next day, it was in a clear sky.

Slowly everything fell into the peaceful order of obedience. With the obedience came an increase of freedom. The steps of the younger members of the family were heard on the stairs and in the hallways, more light and quick than ever before. Their brother had lost the frightening appearance caused by his imprisonment, and his commands were given more gently, and oftener with a smile, than ever before. Gradually his presence was felt throughout the house. It was no surprise to anyone at his studies to see the oldest brother by his side when he lifted up his eyes, though he had not before known that he was in the room. And although some dread still remained, it was quickly disappearing as a firm friendship grew. Without immediately ordering their work, he always influenced them, and often changed their direction and goals. The change soon evident in the household was remarkable. A simpler, nobler expression could be seen on all the faces. The voices of the men were deeper, and yet seemed by their very depth more tender than before; while the voices of the women were softer and sweeter, and at the same time richer and more confident.

One of the brothers was very fond of astronomy. He had his observatory on a lofty tower, which stood pretty clear of the others, toward the north and east. Up until then, his astronomy, as he had called it, had been more of the character of astrology. But now he worked from morning to night in the study of the laws of the stars. He learned what law and order and truth are, what agreement and harmony mean. Thus he stood on the earth, and looked to the heavens.

Another had loved to search out the hollow places and nooks in the foundation of the castle, and he was often found with compass and ruler working away at a map he had been in the process of making. But now he came to the conclusion that only by climbing into the upper part of his home could he understand what lay beneath. He decided that, in all probability, one clear look from the top of the highest tower he could reach would show him more about how it was built than a year spent in wandering through its underground chambers. In fact, the desire to go up made him forget what was beneath. He laid aside his chart for a time at least, and his brothers and sisters saw him searching upward, now in one direction, now in another; and seeking, as he went, the best views into the clear air outside.

They all began to find that they were thinking about different parts of the same thing. They brought together their discoveries and recognized the similarities between them. The one thing often explained the other, and combining with it helped them discover something else. They grew more and more friendly and loving so that every now and then one turned to another and said, as in surprise, "Why, you are my brother!" or "Why, you are my sister!" And yet they had always known it.

The change reached to all. One, who was almost always seated by her harp or some other instrument, had, until the late storm, been generally merry and playful, though sometimes sad. But for a long time after that, she was often weeping, and playing little simple tunes which she had heard in childhood. Before long, however, her music became more wild, and sometimes kept its sadness, but it was mixed with hope.

As to the oldest sister, it was many days before she recovered from the shock. Finally, one day, her brother came to her, took her by the hand, led her to an open window, and told her to seat herself by it, and look out. She did so and at first saw nothing more than a blaze of sunlight. But as she looked, the horizon widened out, and the dome of the sky rose, until the splendor held her soul, and she fell on her knees and wept. Now the heavens seemed to bend lovingly over her, and to stretch out wide cloud-arms to embrace her. The earth lay like the chest of a never-ending love beneath her, and the wind kissed her cheek with a scent of roses. She sprang to her feet and turned, expecting to see the face of her father. But there stood only her brother, looking calmly and lovingly on her. She turned again to the window. On the hilltops rested the sky: Heaven and Earth were one; and the prophecy awoke in her soul, that from between them would the steps of the father draw near.

Until then she had seen only Beauty; now she saw Truth. Often had she looked on such clouds as these, and loved the strange curves into which the winds shaped them. She had smiled as her little sister told her what animals she saw in them, and tried to point them out to her. Now they were like troops of angels, thrilled over her new birth, for they sang in her soul, of beauty, and truth, and love. She looked down, and her little sister knelt beside her.

The youngest was a curious child, with black, glittering eyes, and dark hair; a playful, daring girl, who laughed more than she smiled. She was generally with her oldest sister, and was always finding and bringing her strange things. She never pulled a primrose, but she knew the homes of all the orchids and brought from them bees and butterflies, as offerings to her sister. Interesting moths and glow-worms were her greatest delight, and she loved the stars, because they were like the glow-worms. But the change had affected her too. Her sister saw that her eyes had lost their glittering look, and had become more clear. And she saw that her little sister's merriment was more gentle, her smile more frequent. Although she was as wild as ever, there was more elegance in her motions, and more music in her voice. And she clung to her sister with greater fondness than before.

The land rested in the embrace of the warm summer days. The clouds nestled around the towers of the castle, and the hearts of those who lived there became aware of a warm atmosphere—a presence of love. They began to feel like the children of a household when the mother is at home. They grew daily more and more beautiful, until they wondered as they looked at each other. As they walked in the gardens of the castle, or in the country around, they were often visited, especially the oldest sister, by sounds that no one heard but themselves, coming from woods and waters; and by forms of love that lightened out of flowers, and grass, and great rocks. Now and then the young children would come in with a slow, dignified step, and, with great eyes that looked as if they would gulp down all the creation, say that they had met their father among the trees, and that he had kissed them. "And," added one of them once, "I grew so big!" But when the others went out to look, they could see no one. And some said it must have been the brother, who grew more and more beautiful, and loving, and respected. He had lost all traces of hardness, so that they wondered how they could ever have thought him strict and cruel.

Often, at sunrise, their hymn of praise to their unseen father could be heard. They felt him near, though they saw him not. Some of the words once reached my ear through the folds of the music in which they floated, as in a snowstorm of sweet sounds. There was much I seemed to hear which I could not understand, and some things which I understood but cannot speak again. These are some of the words I heard:

We thank you that we have a father, and not a maker; that you have given life to us, and not molded us as images of clay. We have come out of your heart instead of from your hands. It must be so. Only the heart of a father is able to create. We rejoice in it, and bless you that we know it. We thank you for yourself. Be what you are—our root and life, our beginning and end, our all in all. Come home to us. You live; therefore we live. In your light we see. You are—that is all our song.

In this way they worship, and love, and wait. Their hope grows ever stronger and brighter, that one day, before long, the Father will show Himself among them, and from then on live in His own house forevermore. What was once only an old legend has become the one desire of their hearts.

And the highest hope is the surest of being fulfilled.

TWENTY

The Loveliest Rose in the World

by Hans Christian Andersen

(1852)

There lived once a great queen, in whose garden were found at all seasons the most splendid flowers, and from every land in the world. She especially loved roses, and she owned the most beautiful kinds of this flower, from the wild hedge-rose, with its apple-scented leaves, to the splendid Provence rose. They grew near the shelter of the walls, wound themselves around columns and window-frames, crept along passages and over the ceilings of the halls. They were of every fragrance and color.

But worry and sorrow lived within these halls, because the queen lay sick, and the doctors said that she would die. "There is still one thing that could save her," said one of the wisest among them. "Bring her the loveliest rose in the world; one which shows the purest and brightest love. If it is brought to her before her eyes close, she will not die."

Then from all parts came those who brought roses that bloomed in every garden, but they were not the right kind. The flower must be one from the garden of love, but which of the roses there showed the highest and purest love? The poets sang of this rose, the loveliest in the world, and each named one which he considered worthy of that title. The request for such a rose was sent far and wide to every heart that beat with love; to every class, age, and condition.

"No one has yet named the flower," said the wise man. "No one has pointed out the spot where it blooms in all its splendor. It is not a rose from the coffin of young lovers, or from the grave of a hero who died for his country. Neither is it the magic flower of Science, obtained by a man who devotes many hours of his life in sleepless nights, in a lonely chamber."

"I know where it blooms," said a happy mother, who came with her lovely child to the bedside of the queen. "I know where the loveliest rose in the world is. It is seen on the blooming cheeks of my sweet child, when it is refreshed by sleep and opens its eyes to smile on me with love."

"This is a lovely rose," said the wise man, "but there is one still more lovely."

"Yes, one far more lovely," said one of the women. "I have

seen it, and a grander and purer rose does not bloom. But it was white, like the leaves of a blush-rose. I saw it on the cheeks of the queen. She had taken off her golden crown, and through the long, dreary night, she carried her sick child in her arms. She wept over it, kissed it, and prayed for it as only a mother can pray in that hour of her suffering."

"Holy and wonderful is the white rose of grief, but it is not the one we seek."

"No, the loveliest rose in the world I saw at the Lord's table," said the good old minister. "I saw it shine as if an angel's face had appeared. A young maiden knelt at the altar and renewed the vows made at her baptism. And there were white roses and red roses on the blushing cheeks of that young girl. She looked up to heaven with an expression of the highest and purest love."

"May she be blessed!" said the wise man. "But no one has yet named the loveliest rose in the world."

Then there came into the room a child—the queen's little son. Tears stood in his eyes and glistened on his cheeks. He carried a great book covered in velvet, with silver clasps. "Mother," cried the little boy, "hear what I have read." And the child seated himself by the bedside, and read from the book about Him who suffered death on the cross to save all people, even who are yet unborn. He read, "Greater love has no man than this," and as he read a rosy color spread over the cheeks of the queen. Her eyes became so bright and clear

that she saw a lovely rose spring out of the pages of the book—
a sign of Him who shed His blood on the cross.

"I see it," she said. "He who beholds this, the loveliest rose
on earth, shall never die."

TWENTY-ONE
Robin Redbreast

by Selma Lagerlöf

English translation by Velma Swanston Howard (1903)

It happened at that time when our Lord created the world, when He not only made heaven and earth, but all the animals and the plants as well, at the same time giving them their names.

One day, when our Lord sat in His Paradise and painted the little birds, the colors in His paint pot ran out. The goldfinch would have been without color if our Lord had not wiped all His paint brushes on its feathers.

It was then that the donkey got his long ears, because he could not remember the name that had been given him. No sooner had he taken a few steps along the meadows of Paradise than he forgot, and three times he came back to ask his name. At last our Lord grew somewhat impatient, took him by his two ears, and said: "Your name is ass, ass, ass!" And while He said this, our Lord pulled both of his ears that the donkey might hear better, and remember what was said to him.

It was on the same day, also, that the bee was punished.

Now, when the bee was created, it began immediately to gather honey, and the animals and human beings who caught the delicious smell of the honey came and wanted to taste of it. But the bee wanted to keep it all for himself. With his poisonous sting, he pursued every living creature that came near his hive. Our Lord saw this and at once called the bee and punished it.

"I gave you the gift of gathering honey, which is the sweetest thing in all creation," said our Lord, "but I did not give you the right to be cruel to your neighbor. Remember well that every time you sting any creature who desires to taste of your honey you shall surely die!"

Ah, yes! It was at that time that the cricket became blind and the ant missed her wings.

So many strange things happened on that day!

Our Lord sat there and planned and created all day long. Toward evening He thought of making a little gray bird. "Remember your name is robin redbreast," said our Lord to the bird, as soon as it was finished. Then He held it in the palm of His open hand and let it fly.

After the bird had been testing his wings a bit, and had seen something of the beautiful world in which he was destined to live, he became curious to see what he himself was like. He noticed that he was entirely gray, and that the breast was just as gray as all the rest of him. Robin redbreast twisted and turned in every direction as he viewed himself in the mirror of a clear lake, but he couldn't find a single red feather. Then he flew back to our Lord.

Our Lord sat there on His throne. Out of His hands came butterflies that fluttered about His head. Doves cooed on His shoulders. And out of the earth around Him grew the rose, the lily, and the daisy.

The little bird's heart beat heavily with fright, but with easy curves he flew nearer and nearer our Lord until at last he rested on our Lord's hand. Then our Lord asked what the little bird wanted.

"I only want to ask you about one thing," said the little bird.

"What is it that you wish to know?" said our Lord.

"Why should I be called redbreast, when I am all gray, from my beak to the very end of my tail? Why am I called redbreast when I do not have one single red feather?"

The bird looked pleadingly on our Lord with its tiny black eyes. Then he turned his head. About him he saw pheasants all red under a sprinkle of gold dust, cocks with red combs, parrots with marvelous red neck bands, to say nothing about the butterflies, the goldfinches, and the roses! And naturally he thought how little he needed—just one tiny drop of color on his breast—and he, too, would be a beautiful bird. "Why should I be called redbreast when I am so entirely gray?" asked the bird once again, and waited for our Lord to say—Ah! my friend, I see that I have forgotten to paint your breast feathers red, but wait a moment and all shall be done.

But our Lord only smiled a little and said, "I have called you robin redbreast, and robin redbreast shall your name be, but you must earn your red breast feathers." Then our Lord lifted His hand and let the bird fly once more—out into the world.

The bird flew down into Paradise, thinking deeply. What could a little bird like him do to earn for himself red feathers? The only thing he could think of was to make his nest in a prickly bush. He built it in among the thorns in the thick woods. It looked as if he waited for a roseleaf to cling to his throat and give him color.

Countless years had come and gone since that day, which was the happiest in all the world! Human beings had learned to farm the earth and sail the seas. They had gotten clothes and ornaments for themselves, and had long since learned to build big temples and great cities—such as Thebes, Rome, and Jerusalem.

Then there dawned a new day, one that will long be remembered in the world's history. On the morning of this day robin redbreast sat upon a little hill outside of Jerusalem's walls and sang to his young ones, who rested in a tiny nest in a briar bush.

Robin redbreast told the little ones all about that wonderful day of creation, and how the Lord had given names to everything, just as each redbreast had told it, ever since the first redbreast had heard God's word and gone out of God's hand. "And mark you," he ended sorrowfully, "so many years have gone, so many roses have bloomed, so many little birds have come out of their eggs since Creation day, but robin redbreast is still a little gray bird. He has not yet succeeded in gaining his red feathers."

The young ones opened wide their tiny bills, and asked if their forebears had never tried to do any great thing to earn the priceless red color.

"We have all done what we could," said the little bird, "but we have all gone wrong. The first robin redbreast one day met another bird exactly like himself, and he began to love it with such a mighty love that he could feel his breast glow. Ah! he thought then, *now I understand! It was our Lord's meaning that I should love so deeply that my breast should grow red in color from the very warmth of the love that lives in my heart.* But he missed it, as all those who came after him have missed it, and as even you shall miss it."

The little ones twittered, utterly bewildered, and began to mourn because the red color would not come to beautify their downy gray breasts.

"We had also hoped that song would help us," said the grown-up bird, speaking in long-drawn-out tones. "The first robin redbreast sang until his breast swelled within him, he was so carried away—and he dared to hope anew. *Ah!* he thought, *it is the glow of the song which lives in my soul that will color my breast feathers red.* But he missed it, as all the others have missed it, and as even you shall miss it." Again was heard a sad "peep" from the young ones' half-naked throats.

"We had also counted on our courage and our valor," said the bird. "The first robin redbreast fought bravely with other birds until his breast flamed with the pride of victory. *Ah!* he thought, *my breast feathers shall become red from the love of battle which burns in my heart.* He too missed it, as all those who came after him have missed it, and as even you shall miss it." The young ones peeped courageously that they still wished to try and win the much-sought-after prize, but the bird answered them sorrowfully that it would be impossible. What could they do when so many splendid relatives had missed the mark? What could they do more than love, sing, and fight? What could—

The little bird stopped short in the middle of the sentence, for out of one of Jerusalem's gates marched a crowd of people. The whole procession rushed up towards the hill where the bird had its nest. There were riders on proud horses, soldiers with long spears, executioners with nails and hammers. There were judges and priests in the procession, weeping women, and above all a mob of mad, loose people running about—a filthy, howling mob of loiterers.

The little gray bird sat trembling on the edge of his nest. He feared each instant that the little briar bush would be trampled down and his young ones killed!

"Be careful!" he cried to the little helpless young ones. "Creep together and stay quiet. Here comes a horse that will ride right over us! Here comes a warrior with iron-clad sandals! Here comes the whole wild, storming mob!" Immediately the bird ceased his cry of warning and grew calm and quiet. He almost forgot the danger hovering over him. Finally he hopped down into his nest and spread his wings over the young ones.

"Oh! This is too terrible," he said. "I don't want you to see this awful sight! There are three criminals who are going to be crucified!" And he spread his wings so the little ones could see nothing.

They caught only the sound of hammers, the cries of pain and the wild shrieks of the mob.

Robin redbreast followed the whole scene with his eyes, which grew big with terror. He could not take his glance from the three unfortunate men.

"How terrible human beings are!" said the bird after a little while. "It isn't enough that they should nail these poor creatures to a cross, but they must place a crown of piercing thorns on the head of one of them. I see that the thorns have wounded his brow so that the blood flows," he continued. "And this man is so beautiful—and he looks about him with such kind glances that everyone ought to love him. I feel as if an arrow were shooting through my heart when I see him suffer!"

The little bird began to feel a stronger and stronger pity for the thorn-crowned sufferer. *Oh! if I were only my brother the eagle*, he thought, *I would draw the nails from his hands, and with my strong claws I would drive away all those who torture him.* He saw how the blood trickled down from the forehead of the crucified one, and he could no longer stay quiet in his nest. *Even if I am little and weak, I can still do something for this poor tortured one*, thought the bird. Then he left his nest and flew out into the air, making wide circles around the crucified one. He flew about him several times without coming near, for he was a shy little bird who had never dared to go near a human being. But little by little he gained courage, flew close to him, and pulled with his little beak a thorn that had become stuck in the forehead of the crucified one. And as he did this there fell on his breast a drop of blood from the face of the crucified one. It spread quickly and colored all the little thin breast feathers.

Then the crucified one opened his lips and whispered to the bird: "Because of your compassion, you have won all that your kind have been struggling to get ever since the world was created."

As soon as the bird had returned to his nest his young ones cried to him, "Your breast is red; your breast feathers are redder than the roses!"

"It is only a drop of blood from the poor man's forehead," said the bird. "It will vanish as soon as I bathe in a pool or a clear well."

But no matter how much the little bird bathed, the red color did not vanish. And when his little ones grew up, the blood-red color shone also on their breast feathers, just as it shines on every robin redbreast's throat and breast until this very day.

A Message to Parents and Teachers

Why Do We Need Fairy Tales and Fantasy?

A decree went throughout all the land that families and schools should protect children from the world of "make-believe." Instead of fairy tales and folk tales, children should hear and read only realistic stories. Their young minds would be trained for clear, rational thinking instead of silly sentimentalism and superstition. Their attention would be focused on practical ways to make their world a better place through hard work and cooperation. When they needed inspiration, it would come from biographies about real men and women of courage and achievement.

One of the thousands of parents who followed this new approach kept a diary of her son's response from birth until the age of seven. She carefully guarded the little boy from all fantasy and encouraged his development with stories about the real world. Instead of seeing her child become clear-thinking with both feet planted firmly on the ground, day after day she watched him sail away into his own fantasy world. He had an imaginary friend, saw a red elephant in his room, and told his mom that the rug was a ship. The child was not mentally ill or emotionally unbalanced; he was simply doing what children do naturally—exercising his gift of imagination. And all the laws and regimes of early Soviet Russia could not suppress this God-given ability to reach beyond the material world.[1]

Similar efforts to suppress fantasy literature have been attempted in many different cultures and centuries. During the seventeenth century, America's leading Puritan minister, Cotton Mather, called fiction "Satan's library," and England's Puritan scholar Richard Baxter included among his past sins that as an adolescent he was "extremely bewitched with a Love of Romances, Fables and old Tales." John Bunyan similarly admitted a youthful enchantment with fantasy literature:

> The Scriptures, thought I, what are they? a dead letter, a little Ink and Paper, of three or four Shillings price. . . . Give me a Ballad, a Newsbook, George on Horseback, or Bevis of Southampton [an adventure

story about a brave knight who married a Saracen princess]. Give me some book that teaches curious Arts, but for the holy Scriptures I cared not.

When Bunyan was converted and became a Baptist minister, his attitude toward the Bible changed completely. He devoted himself to writing and delivering sermons until a change in the political climate sent him to prison. During his second jail term, he looked beyond the walls of his cell into a land of adventure. A story took shape in his mind like a dream, and the result was *The Pilgrim's Progress*. In Bunyan's allegory, the knight Sir Bevis was transformed into the pilgrim Christian, who must also face enemies and danger to reach his goal.

When John Bunyan showed his fanciful story to his friends, many of them advised him against publishing it. They didn't trust this mingling of Christian truth and creative imagination. Fortunately, Bunyan decided to go ahead and give his story to the public, and it captured the hearts and minds of millions of readers as he hoped it would. He was proved correct in his belief that he could use metaphor and allegory to, in his words, make truth's golden beams cast forth its rays as light as day.[2] He also demonstrated that fantasy is not something we outgrow; it is a lifelong means of breaking through the barriers of time, place, and matter in order to glimpse spiritual realities.

Major Benefits of Fantasy Literature

It would be irresponsible to represent all fairy tales and folklore as beneficial to readers. As Wheaton College (Illinois) professor of literature Leland Ryken observes, "Too many modern scholars and enthusiasts for the arts attribute inherent and magical and even religious power to myth, ritual and fantasy *in themselves*. From a Christian perspective this is nonsense. . . . Like anything else in life, the imagination can be either good or bad, redemptive or depraved." [3]

However, conscientious research by educators and psychologists and parents reveals some key reasons that children need fantasy tales of moral and literary excellence.

1. **They stimulate imagination and creativity.** Through storytelling and reading, we can enrich a child's fantasy life, pointing the imagination in life-affirming directions. We have the opportunity to help children understand that human creativity is a reflection of the supreme Creator's power. God invites His children to share in the delight of making new worlds. J. R. R. Tolkien, creator of the hobbits and Middle Earth, wrote, "We make in our measure and in our derivative mode, because we are made: and not only made, but made in the image and likeness of a Maker." [4]

2. **They help readers empathize with others and develop compassion.** When a typically egocentric child

reads a book like *Charlotte's Web*, he is captured in the silken strands of a story about a spider who saves the life of a fat little pig by spinning words of praise about him into her web. When older children read *A Wrinkle in Time*, they discover through Meg how important it is to move beyond not hating enemies to actually caring for them. Fantasy stories have a special ability to lift us out of ourselves and into other people's shoes.

3. **They carry readers beyond the restrictions of time and space and promote a sense of mystery and transcendence.** As Tolkien said, fairy tales "open a door on Other Time, and if we pass through, though only for a moment, we stand outside our own time, outside Time itself, maybe." Clifton Fadiman, book lover and editor, compiled *A World Treasury of Children's Literature*, and in the process accumulated a personal library of approximately 2,000 books from seventy countries. "Why is fantasy a favorite genre in children's literature?" he asked, answering, "Surely in part because it is rooted in the notion of transformation. . . . As children we are princes in disguise; we are stones and plants, beasts and winds; we are jet planes and jet pilots; we are the toys in a shop, we are the shop, we are the shopkeeper; we are the dancer and the dance." [5] As we consider the inborn longing

for escape from the prison bars of earthly existence, we are reminded of the words of Ecclesiastes: God "has set eternity in the hearts of men; yet they cannot fathom what God has done from beginning to end."

4. **They satisfy the innate desire for communion with other living things.** In an age of technology and urban living, they bring readers closer to nature and its Creator. Experts on fantasy literature note that the current surge of interest in fairies and fantasy parallels a similar trend during the Industrial Revolution of the nineteenth century. During times of social upheaval, surrounded by material things, we feel more keenly our loss of the Garden. There is a longing for a world where the lion can lie down by the lamb and we can, in the words of Dr. Dolittle, talk and walk with the animals.

5. **They show how the small and powerless can triumph through perseverance and patience.** In *The Lord of the Rings*, a comfort-loving creature named Frodo is given an overwhelming task. When he protests that he is not equal to it, the wizard Gandalf tells him, "This quest may be attempted by the weak with as much hope as the strong. Yet such is oft the course of deeds that move the wheels of the world: small hands do them because they must while the eyes of the great are elsewhere." This is a frequently recurring theme in fairy tales. We draw courage as we

see ordinary, flawed characters make heroic choices.

6. **They awaken higher ideals without preaching.** Andrew Lang, one of the best-known collectors of fairy tales, said that the main question children ask is "Is it true?" Tolkien countered with the observation that "far more often they have asked me: 'Was he good? Was he wicked?' That is, they were more concerned to get the Right side and the Wrong side clear. For that is a question equally important in History and Faerie."[6] Fantasy worlds, when created with integrity, do not deny or gloss over the reality of evil and human weakness. For instance, in *The Lion, the Witch and the Wardrobe* by C. S. Lewis, Edmund's decision to conspire with the White Witch has far-reaching consequences that are not easily or painlessly reversed. Edmund complained, when he was still secretly siding with the Witch for his own gain, "Which is the right side?" But deep down he really knew. And eventually he was named "the Just" for his ability to know and do what was right. A fantasy that keeps faith with the reader leaves the promise of growing up to be a beautiful swan, of having cinders and shame replaced by royal splendor, and even of having beastliness tamed and transformed by love.

7. **They help readers envision a better society where intelligence, courage, and compassion prevail.** Out-

standing children's author Lloyd Alexander writes, "Fantasy touches our deepest feelings and in so doing, it speaks to the best and most hopeful parts of ourselves." [7] That is why writers often use fairy tales as a means of exposing a society's false values. For instance, in "The Emperor's New Clothes," by Hans Christian Andersen, readers can laugh at the folly and pride of the Emperor, who believes he is resplendently dressed when he is actually naked, and at the people who refuse to admit his error. It is the kind of story that subtly pricks our conscience and brings life into sharper focus. George MacDonald, author of some of our best-loved fairy tales, once said, "If I can wake in any human heart just a little fluttering of life, if I can help any human soul to feel . . . that there is an eternal world, a world of life, of truth; a world of duty, of hope, of infinite joy. . . . If I can make the clouds just part the least bit, and give a glimpse of the blue sky, of the infinite realities of things, then I hold that it is worth doing."

Helping Children Explore Fairy Tales and Fantasy

C. S. Lewis credited George MacDonald's fantasy stories with baptizing his imagination. As an adult concerned with children's spiritual development, you may find the following suggestions helpful in the process of capturing the imagination for Christ.

Share your favorite stories with children, and talk about what makes them special to you. Ask children to share their favorites with you, encouraging them to identify what it is they like about each story or novel. As you become more aware of what appeals to a child, you will become better equipped to direct him or her to books of excellence that satisfy specific interests and attractions.

Provide a wide variety of reading choices and allow the child to identify his or her favorite styles and authors. *Faerie Gold* and other anthologies offer an introduction to many authors of inspirational fantasy literature. You'll find a wealth of book suggestions, along with further insights about fantasy literature, in our book *How to Grow a Young Reader* (Shaw Books, 2002).

Read aloud and listen to audiobooks so that you and your children can experience the wonder and magic of the spoken word. As George MacDonald said, "The very brooding of a voice on a word seems to hatch something of what is in it." Some audiobooks are highly sophisticated productions, and others are more like a parent reading to his or her children. Experiment to find which approach appeals most to your children. Public libraries offer some children's books on tape. In addition, tapes may be rented from many talking-book providers (Books on Tape, Listening Library, and Blackstone—all with Internet Web sites) or purchased in children's bookstores or the children's department of large bookstores, as well as in some used bookstores. In recent years, several companies have launched what is often referred to as "theater for the ear." The BBC (British Broadcasting Corporation) started BBC Radio Presents with four classic audio dramatizations including *The Hobbit.* This classic and other dramatic literary presentations are available now on tape. Focus on the Family Radio Theatre's award-winning productions include *The Lion, the Witch and the Wardrobe, The Horse and His Boy,* and *The Magician's Nephew,* all part of C. S. Lewis's Chronicles of Narnia, and *The Secret Garden* by Frances Hodgson Burnett.

If a child doesn't find fairy tales appealing, don't attempt to force-feed them. Some children enjoy fantasy stories from an early age, and others have to grow into them. C. S. Lewis seems to have been one of the former and, as well as reading and enjoying fantasies, as a boy created his own talking-animal tales. Tolkien, on the other hand, had no special fondness for fairy tales until he was a young adult. His growing love of language as the vehicle of literature and culture, along with the horror of World War I, awakened his deep longing for the Kingdom of Faerie. A child may be too young for fairy tales, but he can never be too old for them.

As you share the world of fairy tales with children, beware of subjecting stories to in-depth analysis or overt moralizing. Don't point out what is "real" and what is "pretend." A microscope and flashlight are the wrong tools to use in the land of wonder. Enjoy the starlight and moonbeams and allow time to reflect on the hidden truths; as much as possible let the tales speak for themselves. If you occasionally share insights you gained from reading, the young reader is apt to share similar personal insights with you . . . when she is ready.

Often children are drawn to less than desirable fantasy stories because "everyone" is reading them. Their interest has less to do with literary appreciation than with peer-group acceptance. In these cases, if you feel you must restrict a young child from a particular book or author, provide simple, clear reasons. As children mature, it is best to go ahead and read the questionable books as a family, discussing key issues of moral concern. If at all possible, follow this reading experience with a book that offers some of the same appealing elements but is of better spiritual value.

"The true meaning of the word 'faerie' is spiritual," as beloved children's author Kate Douglas Wiggins wrote, "but many stories masquerade under that title which have no claim to it. Some universal spiritual truth underlies the really fine old fairy tale; but there can be no educative influence in the so-called fairy stories which are merely jumbles of impossible incidents, and which not infrequently present dishonesty, deceit, and cruelty in amusing guise."[8] Our high calling as adults is to sprinkle a trail of bread crumbs or light a candle that will lead children toward good fairy stories, the kind Tolkien described as higher and more complete, where "however wild its events, however fantastic or terrible the adventures, it can give to child or man that hears it, when the 'turn' comes, a catch of the breath, a beat and lifting of the heart, near to (or indeed accompanied by) tears . . . a piercing glimpse of joy, and heart's desire." [9] And, of course, it is this taste of joy and desire that draws us ever onward to the most incredible, true, and wonder-filled of all stories—the gospel.

Notes

1. Reported by Kornei Chukovsky in *From Two to Five* (1928), translated by Mirian Morton (Berkeley: University of California Press, 1963), 119. Chukovsky's poems and fairy tales for children are now considered classics of Russian literature and have earned him the title of "Russia's Dr. Seuss."
2. Batson, Beatrice. *A Reader's Guide to Religious Literature* (Chicago: Moody Press, 1968), 52–61.
3. Ryken, Leland. *Triumphs of the Imagination: Literature in Christian Perspective* (InterVarsity Press, 1979).
4. Tolkien, J. R. R. "On Fairy-Stories," *Essays Presented to Charles Williams* (Grand Rapids: Eerdmans, 1966), 72.
5. Fadiman, Clifton. "A Meditation on Children and Their Literature," in *Sharing Literature with Children* by Francelia Butler (New York: David McKay, 1977), 477–78.
6. Tolkien, *Essays Presented to Charles Williams*, 63.
7. Alexander, Lloyd. "Fantasy and the Human Condition," *New Advocate* (Spring 1983).
8. Wiggins, Kate Douglas and Nora A. Smith. *The Story Hour: A Book for the Home and Kindergarten* (Boston: Houghton, Mifflin, 1890), introduction.
9. Tolkien, *Essays Presented to Charles Williams*, 81–82.

Great Thoughts about Faerie and Fantasy

A Quotation Collection

When the first baby laughed for the first time, the laugh broke into a thousand pieces and that was the beginning of fairies.

—J. M. Barrie, *Peter Pan*

"Have you seen any fairies lately?" I asked the question of a little girl not long ago. "Huh! There's no such thing as fairies," she replied. In some way the answer hurt me, and I have been vaguely disquieted when I have thought of it ever since. . . . Have you seen any fairies lately, or have you allowed the harsher facts of life to dull your "seeing eye"?

—Laura Ingalls Wilder

Fairyland is a place of perception where the marvelous lies hidden in the mundane.

—George MacDonald, *William Raeper*

If you want your children to be intelligent, read them fairy tales. If you want them to be more intelligent, read them more fairy tales.

—Albert Einstein

When I examine myself and my methods of thought, I come to the conclusion that the gift of fantasy has meant more to me than any talent for abstract, positive thinking.

—Albert Einstein

This excursion into the preposterous sends us back with renewed pleasure to the actual.

—C. S. Lewis, in his review of *The Lord of the Rings*

If you are tired of the real landscape look at it in a mirror. By putting bread, gold, horse, apple, or the very roads into a myth, we do not retreat from reality: we rediscover it. As long as the story lingers in our mind, the real things are more themselves.

—C. S. Lewis, in his review of *The Lord of the Rings*

A fairytale, dear sir, in relating miraculous happenings as though they were the normal events of everyday is a humble acknowledgment of the fact that this universe is a box packed full of mysteries. . . . Heaven alone knows what will pop out of it next.

—Elizabeth Goudge, *The Blue Hills*

Notwithstanding the beauty of this country of Faerie, in which we are, there is much that is wrong in it. If there are great splendors, there are corresponding horrors; heights and depths; beautiful women and awful fiends; noble men and weaklings. All a man has to do, is to better what he can. And if he can settle it with himself, that even renown and success are in themselves of no great value, and be content to be defeated, if so be that the fault is not his; and so go to his work with a cool brain and a strong will, he will get it done; and fare none the worse in the end, that he was not burdened with provision and precaution.

—George MacDonald, *Phantastes*

The realm of fairy story is wide and deep and high and filled with many things: all manner of beasts and birds are found there; shoreless seas and stars uncounted; beauty that is an enchantment, and an everpresent peril; both joy and sorrow as sharp as swords. In that realm a man may, perhaps, count himself fortunate to have wandered, but its very richness and strangeness tie the tongue of a traveler who would re-port them. And while he is there it is dangerous for him to ask too many questions, lest the gates should be shut and the keys be lost.

—J. R. R. Tolkien, "On Fairy Stories"

Do you think I am trying to weave a spell? Perhaps I am; but remember your fairy tales. Spells are used for breaking en-chantments as well as for inducing them. And you and I have need of the strongest spells that can be found to wake us from the evil enchantment of worldliness which has been laid upon us for nearly a hundred years.

—C. S. Lewis, "The Weight of Glory"

If you happen to read fairy tales, you will observe that one idea runs from one end of them to the other—the idea that peace and happiness can only exist on some condition. This idea, which is the core of ethics, is the core of the nursery-tales.

—G. K. Chesterton, *All Things Considered*

Nobody can write a new fairy tale; you can only mix up and dress up the old, old stories, and put the characters into new dresses.

—Andrew Lang, Introduction to *The Lilac Fairy Book*

At all ages, if [fantasy and myth] is used well by the author and meets the right reader, it has the same power: to generalize while remaining concrete, to present in palpable form not concepts or even experiences but whole classes of experience, and to throw off irrelevancies. But at its best it can do more; it can give us experiences we have never had and thus, instead of "commenting on life," can add to it.

—C.S. Lewis, "Sometimes Fairy Stories May Say
Best What's to Be Said," from *Of Other Worlds*

The gospel does have many of the earmarks of a fairy tale. In fairy tales you have the poor boy who becomes rich, the leaden cabinet which turns out to have the treasure in it, the ugly duckling who turns out to be a swan, the frog who becomes a prince. Then we come to the gospel, where it's the Pharisees, the good ones, who turn out to be the villains. It's the whores and tax collectors who turn out to be the good ones. Just as in fairy tales, there is the impossible happy ending when Cinderella does marry the prince, and the ugly duckling is transformed into a swan, so Jesus is not, in the end, defeated. He rises again. In all these ways there is a kind of fairy tale quality to the gospel, with the extraordinary difference, of course, that this is the fairy tale that claims to be true. The difference is that this time it's not just a story being told—it's an event. It did happen! Here's a fairy tale come true.

—Frederich Buechner, interview in *The Door*

In a utilitarian age, of all other times, it is a matter of grave importance that fairy tales should be respected.

—Charles Dickens

Independently of the curious circumstance that such tales should be found existing in very different countries and languages, which augurs a greater poverty of human invention than we would have expected, there is also a sort of wild fairy interest in them, which makes me think them fully better adapted to awaken the imagination and soften the heart of childhood than the good-boy stories which have been in later years composed for them.

—Sir Walter Scott, letter to Edgar Taylor, 1823

The recollection of such reading as had delighted him in his infancy, made him always persist in fancying that it was the only reading which could please an infant. "Babies do not want (said he) to hear about babies; they like to be told of giants and castles, and of somewhat which can stretch and stimulate their little minds."

—Mrs. Thrale, *Anecdotes of Samuel Johnson*

There are worlds beyond worlds and times beyond times, all of them true, all of them real, and all of them (as children know) penetrating each other.

—P. L. Travers, author of *Mary Poppins*

Oh! Give us once again the wishing-cup
Of Fortunatus, and the invisible coat
Of Jack the Giant-Killer, Robin Hood,
And Sabra in the forest with St. George!
The child, whose love is here, at least, doth reap
One precious gain, that he forgets himself.
—William Wordsworth, *The Prelude*

I think what profess to be realistic stories for children are far more likely to deceive them [than fantasy stories]. I never expected the real world to be like the fairy tales. I think that I did expect school to be like school stories. The fantasies did not deceive me: the school stories did.
—C. S. Lewis, "On Three Ways of Writing for Children"

Often it is the most obviously fantastic literature that touches most powerfully and at the most points on actual experience.
—Leland Ryken, *Triumphs of the Imagination*

Fantasy touches our deepest feelings and in so doing, it speaks to the best and most hopeful parts of ourselves.
—Lloyd Alexander, "Fantasy and the Human Condition," from *New Advocate*

I like nonsense—it wakes up the brain cells. Fantasy is a necessary ingredient in living. It's a way of looking at life through the wrong end of a telescope . . . and that enables you to laugh at all of life's realities.

—Dr. Seuss, Theodore Geisel

The way to read a fairy tale is to throw yourself in.

—W. H. Auden

By confining your child to blameless stories of child life in which nothing at all alarming ever happens, you would fail to banish the terrors, and would succeed in banishing all that can ennoble them or make them endurable. For in the fairy tales, side by side with the terrible figures, we find the immemorial comforters and protectors, the radiant ones; and the terrible figures are not merely terrible, but sublime. It would be nice if no little boy in bed, hearing or thinking he hears, a sound, were ever at all frightened. But if he is going to be frightened, I think it better that he should think of giants and dragons than merely of burglars. And I think St George, or any bright champion in armour, is a better comfort than the idea of police.

—C. S. Lewis, "On Three Ways of
Writing for Children"

FAERIE GOLD

We cannot say why an egg can turn into a chicken any more than we can say why a bear could turn into a fairy prince. As ideas, the egg and the chicken are further off from each other than the bear and the prince; for no egg in itself suggests a chicken, whereas some princes do suggest bears.

—G. K. Chesterton, "The Ethics
of Elfland," from *Orthodoxy*

Whatever its surface ornamentation, fantasy that strives to reach the level of durable art deals with the bedrock of human emotions, conflicts, dilemmas, relationships. That is to say: the realities of life.

—Lloyd Alexander, Children's Book
Council, "Meet the Author"

It is God who gives you your mirror of imagination, and if you keep it clean, it will give back no shadow but of the truth.

—George MacDonald, *Paul Faber, Surgeon*

The moral imagination is an imagination under discipline— the discipline of faith. It allows the grace of God to cover its failings, but always strives to be under the direction of God. This kind of imagination is a powerful spiritual tool. It helps us see what others do not, and to see more deeply into people and situations, beyond that which the senses can perceive.

—Terry W. Glaspey, *Children of a Greater God*

The immoral imagination gives free rein to every corrupt thought that would enter. . . . Once immoral imagination is awakened, it often leads to sins of thought or deed.

—George MacDonald, *Paul Faber, Surgeon*

The antidote to indulgence is development, not restraint, and that such is the duty of the wise servant of Him who made the imagination.

—George MacDonald,
"The Imagination," from *A Dish of Oats*

Authors Featured in Faerie Gold

Louisa May Alcott (1832–1888)

Louisa May Alcott was born into an unusual family and grew up near Boston. She was surrounded by stimulating people, conversations, ideas, and books—and also by impracticality. Her philosopher father was a dreamer who started a utopian communal farm called Fruitlands. The farm soon fell apart because its transcendental residents liked talking about their philosophies better than farm labor. In spite of her family's hardships, Louisa found outlets for her creativity in writing stories, poems and plays, which she and her sisters presented. One of her greatest joys was taking nature walks with family friend and author Henry David Thoreau.

Louisa was practical as well as artistic. By the time she was seventeen, she had started to take responsibility for her family's financial needs. She hired herself out as a reader to the elderly and ill, cared for little children, and did mending and laundry for other families. At the same time, she persevered in her effort to become a writer. When she was twenty her first poem appeared in a national magazine. Three years later her first book, *Flower Fables*, was published.

In 1862 Louisa served as a Civil War nurse in Washington, D.C. While there she became ill with typhoid fever, and the mercury-tainted medicine the doctors gave her damaged her health for the rest of her life. As soon as she regained enough strength, Louisa resumed her effort to make a living for her family with her pen. Her editor talked her into writing a girl's story. Although Louisa thought the book might be too dull, she agreed. To her surprise *Little Women* was an immediate bestseller. Similar novels followed, all of them enjoying great success. Royalties from her books made it possible for Louisa to support her parents and her orphaned niece, who was like a daughter to her.

Hans Christian Andersen (1805–1875)

Hans Andersen, the son of a poor Danish washerwoman and a shoemaker, was often ridiculed and mistreated by his peers. His deep love of children and concern for their suffering is clear in his *Fairy Tales*. Although he loved books and the theater from childhood and dreamed of becoming famous, he was "the Ugly Duckling"—a failure in the trades his mother chose for him, and as an actor, singer, and dancer. His determination to make something of his life won him a sponsor and an education. He made a fairly successful beginning as a poet and novelist. Then in 1835 he wrote four short stories for the daughter of the secretary of the Academy of Art. The Ugly Duckling at last had become a Beautiful Swan.

In the next forty years, Andersen wrote more than 150 stories for children, and they have been translated into more than eighty languages. His early stories were based on old folktales, but around 1843 he began to create his own stories. His frequent travels, love of nature, memories of childhood, and everyday events became the "seeds" for his fairy tales. "They lay in my thoughts as a seed-corn," he said, "requiring only a flowing stream, a ray of sunshine, a drop from the cup of bitterness, for them to spring forth and burst into bloom."

Andersen's *Fairy Tales* are considered to be among the most beautiful, sensitive, and powerful tales ever told. Fancy and reality blend in these stories, which include "The Little Match Girl," "The Ugly Duckling," "The Little Mermaid," "The Emperor's New Clothes," and his masterpiece, "The Snow Queen." His tales contain sweetness and sadness, gravity and sunshine.

Frances Browne (1816–1879)

Born in County Donegal, Ireland to a village postmaster and his wife, Frances became blind at the age of eighteen months as a result of smallpox. She was one of twelve children, and her parents had no money for a private tutor. Frances learned by listening to her brothers and sisters as they repeated their lessons at home in the evenings. Since her family could not afford any books, kind people loaned books to the Browne children. Frances did her brothers' and sisters' chores so they would have time to read to her. Soon she also repaid them with entertaining stories of her own.

Frances started writing poetry when she was seven (dictating poems to family and friends). When she was about fifteen she heard some great classical poetry that made her believe her writing was worthless. She burned her poems and didn't write again for almost ten years. Then she heard simple Irish poems that gave her new hope for her own writing. Soon magazines began to publish her poetry, and in 1844 a book-length collection of her poems was released. This volume earned her fame as "the blind poetess of Donegal" and a yearly pension of twenty pounds from a patron of the arts.

Frances used her earnings as a writer to help one of her sisters get an education. This sister then became Frances's secretary and reader. The two women moved to Edinburgh, where Frances made just enough money to take care of them with a little left over for her mother in Ireland. She worked hard to earn a living, writing stories, essays, song lyrics, and reviews on assignment. In 1852 another distinguished patron of the arts gave her one hundred pounds. This allowed her to move to London and spend more time on the writing she most wanted to do. Of all she wrote, *Granny's Wonderful Chair* is the one enduring favorite.

Dinah Mulock Craik (1826–1887)

From early childhood and through her teens, Dinah Mulock had a difficult life. Her gifted minister father was mentally ill, often unreasonably stubborn and cruel, and unable to provide for his family. Dinah's mother started a school in Newcastle as a source of income, and at age thirteen Dinah became her assistant. When her mother died in 1845, Dinah's father deserted her and her two younger brothers. Dinah took up writing children's books and then adult novels to support herself. Her brothers died tragically, one at sea in 1847 and the other after a long struggle with illness in 1863.

Tall and slender, full of energy, talent, and wit, Dinah enjoyed her life as an independent single woman and successful author. She turned her attention to writing and editing fantasy literature in 1850, and at the request of publisher Alexander Macmillan she compiled a collection of fairy tales, described by him as "the cream of the cream of Fairy lore." In 1865 she married George Lillie Craik. Although George was a Scotsman, the couple made their home in London where he worked for Macmillan's publishing house and Dinah wrote for children and adults. They adopted an abandoned baby girl and named her Dorothy, "the gift of God."

Up until Dinah's death she continued to write, producing twenty novels, a dozen children's books, and hundreds of poems, short stories, and essays. She was a lifelong champion and friend of working women, a best-selling novelist, and admired by many of Britain's most famous writers, including Lord Tennyson and Robert Browning. Her most enduring novel is *The Little Lame Prince* (1875).

Annie Fellows Johnston (1863–1931)

When Annie was two years old, her father, a Methodist minister, died. The rest of her childhood was spent with her mother and two sisters on a farm near Evansville, Indiana. As a girl, Annie started writing poems and stories like the ones she read in magazines. Always an eager reader and student, she began teaching school when she was only seventeen. After a few years of teaching and work as a private secretary, Annie toured New England and Europe, and then came home to marry a widower with three children. William Johnston encouraged his wife's interest in writing, and she sent her stories to various magazines. When he died in 1892, Annie was left to raise her stepchildren alone. That is when her serious career as a writer began. Her first book was published the next year.

In 1895 Annie and her children went to visit relatives in Pewee Valley, Kentucky. She fell in love with the relaxed, elegant style of Southern life. While she was there, she met a little girl who reminded her of an old-time Confederate colonel. When she returned to Evansville, she wrote *The Little Colonel*. It was so successful that she wrote twelve more books in what became a very popular series. In 1898 she moved to Pewee Valley, where she lived until her death, except for a few years in the West where she nursed her stepson through a terminal illness. In 1935 Annie's best-known story came to the silver screen with Shirley Temple as the Little Colonel.

Selma Lagerlöf (1858–1940)

During Selma's childhood in Varmland, a province of southern Sweden, she became enchanted by fairy tales, legends, and adventurous tales of her native land. She began writing poetry as a child. For ten years, she taught school in Landskrona, Sweden. In 1890 she won a Swedish newspaper literary contest for her first novel, which was published the next year. Her next book, a collection of short stories, was an immediate success. In 1895 she won a traveling scholarship and financial help from the Swedish Academy, which allowed her to become a full-time writer.

The National Teachers' Associate of Sweden asked her to write a geographical reader about Sweden, and she spent three years studying the folklore and natural history of the provinces. This resulted in her internationally honored books titled *The Wonderful Adventures of Nils* (1906) and *The Further Adventures of Nils* (1907). In these stories she presents Sweden's climate, landscape, wild creatures, people, and traditions through the experiences of young Nils, a farmer's son. Nils is bad-tempered and unkind to animals. He becomes an elf who rides on the back of a wild goose and is soon enlightened. In Lagerlöf's fantasy stories, good is seen triumphing over evil.

Lagerlöf is remembered as the foremost Swedish novelist of her time. Her novels and short stories show the strong influence of fairy tales and folklore on her creative imagination. In 1909 she was the first woman and the first Swede to receive the Nobel Prize in Literature. Tenderhearted and concerned with the welfare of others, just prior to World War II, she helped German artists and intellectuals escape to Sweden. Then, when Soviet Russia tried to take Finland, she donated her gold Nobel Prize medal to raise money toward Finland's resistance.

Andrew Lang (1844–1912)

Andrew Lang grew up in Scotland and graduated from St. Andrews University. Although he spent much of his adult life in England, his work reflected his love of Scotland. He was a brilliant scholar, historian, and expert in folklore. He believed that people around the world share certain basic human feelings, and he thought this explained why similar stories developed in very different cultures. To support his theory, he collected fairy tales from many lands and ethnic groups. Then he turned to Mrs. Lang and others who retold the stories for children. Thus, Lang actually served as editor for the series known as the Colour Fairy Books that bears his name. The first one was *The Blue Fairy Book* (1889), featuring tales from Grimm and Perrault, old chapbook stories, some selections from *The Arabian Nights*, some Scottish tales, and an abridged version of *Gulliver's Travels*.

Lang wrote in the introduction to *The Pink Fairy Book*:

> We see that black, white, and yellow people are fond of the same kind of adventures. Courage, youth, beauty, kindness, have many trials, but they always win the battle; while witches, giants, unfriendly cruel people, are on the losing side. So it ought to be, and so on the whole it is and will be; and that is the moral of all fairy tales.

His yearly color books, which ended in 1910 with *The Lilac Fairy Book*, branched out and included traditional folklore from all over the world. In addition to collecting fairy tales, Lang wrote several of his own. The best of them is *The Gold of Fairnilee*, based on the Scottish legends and ballads of his childhood.

George MacDonald (1824–1905)

Although George MacDonald was a minister plagued with poverty, illness, and bereavements, he was also a celebrated literary figure and public speaker. He was so spectacular on an 1872 lecture tour in the United States that he was offered the pastorate of a church on New York's Fifth Avenue with a salary of twenty thousand dollars a year. Leading American authors eagerly befriended him.

MacDonald's literary talent can't compare with that of his friend Mark Twain, but his power of imagination makes him at least Twain's equal. In 1873, Twain and his wife visited the MacDonalds in England. From 1876 to 1883 the two authors sometimes exchanged their works. Twain liked George MacDonald, and he and his daughter Susie loved MacDonald's fantasy *At the Back of the North Wind* (1871).

One of MacDonald's greatest gifts was his ability to gently draw his readers' hearts toward God. His fantasies *The Princess and the Goblin* (1872) and *The Princess and Curdie* (1883) are a wonderful pair of stories for readers of any age. They are easy and exciting enough for children and wise enough for elderly professors. Twenty of MacDonald's other stories are available in a two-volume set called *The Gifts of the Child Christ: Fairy Tales and Stories for the Childlike* (Eerdmans, 1973). The favorites in that set are "The Golden Key" and "The Light Princess." MacDonald said, "For my part I do not write for children, but for the childlike, whether five or fifty or seventy-five."

MacDonald was good friends with Lewis Carroll, and Carroll sent his *Alice in Wonderland* manuscript to MacDonald to see how his family would like it. So MacDonald was the first parent in the world to read *Alice* to his children. (He had eleven children of his own and had adopted two more who needed a home.)

C. S. Lewis was strongly influenced by MacDonald's writing. As a Christian he said that he owed more to MacDonald than any other single writer. In *The Great Divorce*, a short fantasy for adults, Lewis pictured himself meeting George MacDonald on the outskirts of heaven and telling the wise old man how his writing had led Lewis to Christianity.

Edith Nesbit (1858–1924)

British author Edith Nesbit knew both wealth and poverty. When she was young her widowed mother lost all her money, and later her husband lost his business capital because of a dishonest partner. She had to support the family herself, which she did in a variety of ways, including hand-coloring Christmas cards and, eventually, writing books for children.

The Treasure Seekers (1899) was her first book and the beginning of a series about the Bastable children. They dig for treasure, sell poems, serve as detectives, rescue a princess, and borrow money. The other two Bastable stories are *The Wouldbegoods* (1901) and *New Treasure Seekers*.

Nesbit wrote a second set of three books about a family of

children who fall into fantastic adventures: *Five Children and It* (1902), *The Phoenix and the Carpet* (1904), and *The Story of the Amulet* (1906). C. S. Lewis mentioned the Bastables at the beginning of his own children's book *The Magician's Nephew*. He was particularly fond of *The Story of the Amulet*.

In 1998 Britain's Royal Mail paid tribute to fantasy literature with a series of stamps entitled "Magical Worlds." The stamps illustrate scenes from *The Hobbit, Through the Looking-Glass, The Lion, the Witch and the Wardrobe*, and *The Borrowers*. In the brochure that accompanied the stamps, Nesbit is credited with opening up the way for real children to step effortlessly between their world and the world of fantasy.

Emilie Poulsson (1853–1939)

Emilie grew up in Newark, New Jersey, the granddaughter of Norwegian and British grandparents. She had poor vision from the time she was a baby, so after finishing public school she enrolled in the famous Perkins Institution for the Blind in South Boston. She also trained to become a kindergarten and elementary-school teacher in Boston. From 1879 through 1882 she taught at the Perkins School. Then she became a private teacher, lecturer, writer, and, in 1897, editor of the *Kindergarten Review*. Her books include *Nursery Finger Plays* (1889), *In the Child's World* (1893), *Through the Farmyard Gate* (1896), *Child Stories and Rhymes* (1898), *Love and Law in Child Training* (1899), *Holiday Songs* (1901), *In the Child's World*

(1919), and *Finger Plays for Nursery and Kindergarten* (1921). She also contributed many articles and poems to magazines, including *Books are keys to wisdom's treasures; Books are gates to lands of pleasure;* and *Books are friends. Come, let us read.*

Katherine Pyle (1863–1938)

Katherine and her older brother Howard were the children of Quakers with deep roots in Delaware's Brandywine Valley. Their parents encouraged their artistic nature by surrounding them with great literature and art. In 1876 Howard sold a story and illustrations about a magic pill to *Scribner's Monthly.* Early the next year his first fairy tale sold to *St. Nicholas Magazine,* the leading children's periodical. Soon he had an invitation to come to New York as a magazine illustrator. In New York City he became well known for his illustrations in *Harper's Weekly* and other major magazines. But by 1879 he was tired of New York and decided to return to his Wilmington studio. After teaching art for several years at Drexel Institute in Philadelphia, Howard opened his own school of art in Wilmington in 1900.

Like her older brother Howard, Katherine Pyle showed an early interest in writing and drawing. Her first published poem appeared in *Atlantic Monthly* during her childhood. As a young woman, she was an art student of Howard's at the Drexel Institute. For a few years she pursued her career in New York, where she wrote her first published book, *The Counterpane*

Fairy (1898). Then, like Howard, she returned to Wilmington, where she spent the rest of her life.

In addition to writing and illustrating her own short stories, poems, and plays for children, she illustrated several books by other authors. Her projects included collections of fairy tales and legends. She believed these stories had tremendous value because they showed readers that eventually good always triumphs. Among her noteworthy books are *The Christmas Angel* (1900), *Once Upon a Time in Delaware* (1911), *Tales of Wonder and Magic* (1920), *Tales from Greek Mythology* (1928), and *Charlemagne and His Knights* (1932). She contributed poems and illustrations for the children's classic *The Wonder Clock: Or Four and Twenty Marvelous Tales* (1887), a favorite for reading aloud.

Along with Katherine's artistic pursuits, she became an advocate for juvenile offenders in Wilmington. She had a strong concern about social reform and gave generously to the needy.

Laura E. Richards (1850–1943)

Laura grew up in Boston, Massachusetts, the daughter of two famous Americans: Julia Ward Howe, who wrote "The Battle Hymn of the Republic," and Dr. Samuel Gridley Howe, founder of the Perkins School for the Blind. In 1871 she married an architect and industrialist, and the couple made their home in Gardiner, Maine. Like her parents, Laura spent much of her time trying to make her world a better place in which to live. When she wasn't working to improve life in Gardiner, she was busy writing and raising her seven children.

Her poems for children seemed to, in her words, "bubble up from some spring of nonsense" deep within her. They kept bubbling from the publication of her first book in 1880 until her final anthology, *Tirra Lira*, in 1932. She also wrote short stories for her own children, which eventually appeared in books, and novels for girls. Her most successful children's book was *Captain January*. She and her sister Maud Howe Elliott won the first Pulitzer Prize given to a biography for their two-volume biography of their mother, *Julia Ward Howe*. Laura believed her best books were *The Golden Windows* (1903) and *The Silver Crown* (1906), both collections of fables.

After years of struggling to keep the family paper mill in operation, the Richardses closed it in 1900 and opened a camp for boys, one of only three in the U.S. at that time. Camp Merryweather (named after the family in one of her book series) helped to nurture many national leaders. In addition, Laura was the literary mentor of a young man who became the famous poet Edwin Arlington Robinson.

Christina Rossetti (1830–1894)

The youngest child of an exiled Italian patriot and a half-Italian mother, Christina Rossetti lived in London her entire life. Her mother homeschooled her and nurtured her in the Christian faith, while her professor father encouraged her artistic interests and abilities. She also gained a great appreciation for nature during frequent visits to the country with her grandfather.

Her two brothers, Dante Gabriel and William, became accomplished artists, and the lovely young Christina often modestly posed for them and their painter friends. While the brothers worked magic on canvas, Christina wrote poetry. When she was seventeen, her grandfather privately published a small collection of her poems. Fifteen years later, when her book *Goblin Market and Other Poems* was published, England began to recognize Christina as a remarkably gifted poet.

Among Christina's many famous friends was Professor Charles Dodgson, better known as Lewis Carroll, the author of *Alice in Wonderland*. After the success of his book, she wrote her small collection of fantasy stories called *Speaking Likenesses*. In a letter to her brother Dante Gabriel, she explained that the children in the stories were constantly encountering "speaking likenesses" (mirror images) of their own faults and character flaws. In this book and many of her other works, her theme was the need to resist temptation through self-discipline, gratitude, and humility.

Much of Christina's writing centered on her deeply personal Christian faith. In spite of poor health, she wrote more than nine hundred poems and books of devotional prose, and worked for various missionary and charitable organizations. Today her name is largely unknown, except in literary circles where she is still recognized as one of the few great women poets of England. However, the words of several of her poems are known by many, especially the following lines from her Christmas Carol:

What can I give Him,
Poor as I am?
If I were a shepherd
I would bring a lamb,
If I were a wise man
I would do my part,—
Yet what I can I give Him,
Give my heart.

Henry Van Dyke (1852–1933)

Henry Jackson Van Dyke was born in Germantown, Pennsylvania, and attended Princeton University in New Jersey. After his graduation in 1873, he became pastor of the Brick Presbyterian Church in New York City. He served as its minister until 1899, when he returned to Princeton as a professor of English literature. Following twenty-four years as an English professor, he became a U.S. ambassador to the Netherlands and Luxembourg, and then moderator of the General Assembly of the Presbyterian Church. He served as chairman of the committee that compiled the Presbyterian *Book of Common Worship* in 1905 and helped with its revision in 1932.

As a hymn writer, he is best known for "Joyful, Joyful, We Adore Thee." He authored many books of sermons, essays, poetry, and inspirational writings. The most widely known of his works are *The Other Wise Man* (1896), a Christmas story, and his translation of German poet Novalis's *The Blue Flower* (1902).